Andy's Mountain

Andy's Mountain

BIANCA BRADBURY

Illustrated by Robert MacLean

1969

HOUGHTON MIFFLIN COMPANY BOSTON

Other Books by

BIANCA BRADBURY

Mutt

One Kitten Too Many

Tough Guy

Jim and His Monkey

Two on an Island

The Three Keys

Dogs and More Dogs

Andy's Mountain

I

"GRAMPS IS WRONG," Andy said.

He and his sister had wandered down the lane because they wanted to talk alone. They were sitting in the little shelter Gramps had built to protect them from the weather, while they waited for the school bus every morning. Ellen's answer, when it came, was a question. "We think he's wrong, but how do we tell him that?"

"I don't know," Andy said, "but we've got to do it."

They listened. Here, where the Wheelers' lane met Mount Tom Road, the giant earthmovers and bulldozers sounded close. Sometimes Ellen and Andy walked across the fields to watch them carving out the new four-lane highway, knocking down and trampling everything in their path.

Ellen hated the machines. At first Andy had been fascinated by them, but now he hated them too. Each yard they moved brought them that much closer to the Wheeler land.

What was going to happen when they reached the edge of Gramps' property?

Their grandmother was scared, the children suspected. "Your grandfather is the most stubborn man in the world," Gram often said. Well, Andy and Ellen had always known that. His stubbornness was a family joke. Even long ago, when they were little kids and came to visit the farm, the family used to laugh about Gramps being "set in his ways."

Their mother and father had brought them often, and Ellen and Andy had learned to love every stick and stone of the old place. When tragedy struck, and their parents were killed in an automobile accident, their grandparents had come to take them home. "Home" was the farm.

Ellen was only five then, and Andy was seven. Andy still remembered everything that happened that awful night, four years ago. They were living in the city. He and his sister had gone to sleep knowing that the baby-sitter was downstairs in the living room, and that their father and mother would be coming home late from the theater. They had awakened hearing the baby-sitter crying, and had put on their bathrobes and gone downstairs.

Policemen were in the hall. Andy still remembered his terror, while they waited. Then Gramps and Gram had come, and helped them dress, and led them out to the car. Andy asked, "Where are we going?" and Gram said, "Home."

Andy knew the land now almost as well as his grandfather did. He had worked it with Gramps, helping as best he could with the plowing and sowing and haying, and taking care of the stock. A small boy couldn't do the work of a hired hand, though, and it had be-

come almost impossible to find good farm workers. Finally, a year ago, the Wheelers had given up, and sold the herd, and gone out of farming.

Andy was thinking so hard about all that, he failed to hear what his sister said. "Huh?" he grunted.

"What's the matter with you? Your wits are wool-gathering. What about the shotgun?" Ellen repeated.

"What about what shotgun? Do you mean the rifle?"

"All right, the rifle. Last night after supper he took it down from the place where it hangs, in the entryway, and he cleaned it. When I went out to the kitchen he asked me for some old rags. He took it all apart on the table, and oiled it."

"So what?" Andy asked. "He always cleans that gun two or three times a year. He's never used it though, except once when he shot a copperhead snake, down by the hen house."

"He says he'll shoot anybody who tries to take his property away from him."

Andy really looked at his sister then, and saw that she was honestly frightened. He remembered seeing that same stony, still look in his grandmother's face lately. "Look," he said, "Gramps is just making noises. We've got to remember that he's getting old. Ye gods, he was seventy-three his last birthday. He sounds kind of crazy sometimes, the things he says, but they don't mean anything."

"What will he do when the machines get to our line? What will he do when the police come to put us out of our house?"

Andy's shoulders suddenly ached, as though the whole weight of the universe had been dumped on his shoulders. "I don't know," he mumbled.

"Aren't you worried?"

Andy considered that. "If you mean am I worried about the way this mess is going to turn out, yes, I guess I am," he said. "If you mean am I worried that Gramps will use his gun on anybody, no, I'm not."

They wandered along the lane toward the house, but Ellen stopped. "We forgot to look in the mailbox," she reminded Andy.

He ran back. He was hoping there wouldn't be an official-looking letter. The Wheelers had learned to dread long, white letters with the words "State Highway Commission" printed in the corner. Andy's luck was in, and he found only a letter from Gram's sister, and a couple of advertising circulars, and a new mail-order catalog.

Mrs. Grabowski, who lived on the next farm, had taken Gram to town to do her marketing. The two women passed the children in the lane. Andy carried in the packages and Ellen put the groceries away.

This was a Friday afternoon, early in May. The following day, Saturday, was circled in red on the calendar, for it marked the opening of the fishing season. Andy and his grandfather had been looking forward to this for a long time, ever since the cold weather and blizzards of January.

When Gramps wiped the mud off his shoes and came in for supper he was really in high spirits. His faded, blue eyes were shining and his back was straighter than ever, and he even danced a couple of steps.

He spotted the mail-order catalog and picked it up and hefted it, then put his arm around Ellen. "There's a grand lot of good reading in this book," he told her. "Maybe you'll find something pretty you'd like your old Gramps to buy for you. Gram is going to pick out the new curtains she's been wanting for the parlor."

Nobody felt like mentioning that if the state went ahead with its plans the family wouldn't need new curtains, because they wouldn't have a house or a parlor to hang curtains in. Ellen just laughed and hugged

Gramps. He was such a happy soul, how could they get mad at him? They didn't even show they worried about him, to his face. They had to do their worrying in private, behind his back.

When Andy went up to bed that night he followed the old man's instructions and laid out warm clothes so he could jump into them fast. He awoke at five to find Gramps standing over him, shining a flashlight into his face. He silently dressed. Gramps had coffee perking, and there was a plate of jelly doughnuts on the table. They ate, and pulled on their boots, picked up their rods and fishing boxes and went outside. The world was just beginning to turn gray.

They couldn't travel to any trout streams that were far away, because Gramps was too old to drive a car now. That didn't matter, though. Mount Tom Brook, one of the best fishing brooks in the state, wound through their own land.

They crossed wide fields and followed a cow path down to the stream. Early as they were, other fishermen were earlier. Andy made out the figures of two men at the bend where the water circled a grove of alders. "Hello, Mr. Wheeler," one of them called. "We figured you'd be along soon."

"Any luck?" Andy asked.

"No, not yet. Even if we hooked on to a big one, though, we'd have to put it back. Your grandfather's supposed to catch the first one, to open the season legally!"

Gramps chuckled. "You city fellers were only waiting for me to show you how it's done."

He and Andy left the men in possession of that stretch of water, and splashed upstream. Dawn was breaking in rosy streaks across the sky when they arrived at their favorite spot. The brook narrowed, running swiftly over the pebbly bottom. Above, rocks formed a pool six feet deep. The two slipped and slid along the muddy bank and reached a grassy, level place.

Andy bent over the water. "Hey, Old Joe, are you down there?" he called.

"He's there, all right," Gramps said contentedly. Old Joe was a legendary fish that lived in the pool. No one but Gramps had ever seen him. If Gramps happened to say anything that sounded like a lie, somebody in the family was sure to remark, "Old Joe told you that."

Casting, where there were so many trees around, required real skill. Andy had learned well, although in the process he had wasted a lot of time untangling his line from branches and bushes. He was aware the old man was watching. With his thumb on the reel catch he carefully swung his arm back, then forward. The line whistled straight over the water and the feather fly settled right where he wanted it. No fish rose to take it, and he reeled in and cast again.

They fished in silence, Gramps standing on rocks, Andy hip-deep in the water. It was their lucky day, and within an hour each had fish in his creel. As always Gramps caught the best, a twelve-inch beauty of a speckled trout.

They left the pool and slogged upstream to visit with other fishermen. The first day of the season was a social occasion as well as a fishing one. Any sportsman was welcome on the Wheeler land, as long as he came to fish. Hunting was forbidden. Gramps didn't allow anyone to shoot over his fields.

They crawled under barbed wire and soon heard talking. Andy recognized one voice as that of his best friend, Bill Otis, who lived down the road at Dog Leg Corner. Bill was fishing with his father and the Repko brothers from town. They all called greetings, and the Otises joined the Wheelers on the bank.

Andy saw why. Mike Repko was a big man, about as graceful as a bull in a china shop. When he cast, his line whistled around wildly, and anybody in its path was likely to get hooked. The four watched him warily. He was a friendly fellow and meant well, but in a trout stream he was a positive menace.

Andy had been enjoying the morning because it was so still. The road crew didn't work on Saturday, so there weren't any machines clanking and growling in the distance. Now Andy was hoping that Mr. Otis wouldn't mention the Wheeler case, for Andy wanted one whole day free of worry.

His hopes were dashed. Bill's father was a lawyer, and naturally he was interested. He kept his eyes on Mr. Repko's lashing fishline as he asked Gramps, "How's your battle with the Highway Department going?"

"Fine," Gramps said cheerfully, "just fine. You don't see any of those Highway fellers on my land, do you?"

Mr. Otis was only half Gramps' age. He was a good lawyer, and took his profession seriously. "Mr. Wheeler, I've told you before but I want to tell you again, you ought to let me represent you," he said earnestly. "It won't cost you a cent. Now isn't that a fair offer?"

"It is," Gramps agreed. "My grandson has asked me time and time again to come to your office and talk to you. My wife's done the same. We all appreciate your wanting to help. I'll promise you one thing, Mr. Otis, if I ever do find myself in a bind where I need a lawyer, you're the one I'll come to."

Andy was disappointed that this day was doing to be ruined by talking about the case. Just the same, he realized that some good might come out of Gramps' meeting Bill's father this way, face-to-face. "Believe me, the rest of us know how much Gramps needs your help, Mr. Otis," he said. "He's just so stubborn he won't listen to anybody."

The lawyer turned to Andy. "I don't believe your grandfather has really thought this thing through. He refuses to admit that the state has the right to condemn the part of his land that they need for the highway. In the end the state will take it. Everything would go easier for your grandfather if he'd give in now, and let me make the best deal I can with the Highway Department."

"I know that, sir," Andy said.

"Well, I don't know any such thing!" Gramps blustered.

Bill had wandered off, and Andy followed him, leaving the two men to talk. He found Bill sitting on the bank and trying to work a backlash out of his line. It was a two-man job to clear the reel and they bent over it, absorbed. Andy could still hear the men's voices, Mr. Otis' earnest and serious, Gramps' light and humorous.

Gramps had such a sunny disposition, he had a hard time working up a real rage. That was why his family couldn't understand his intense hatred for the Highway Department.

"Your grandfather is never going to give in," Bill mentioned.

All Andy wanted to do was drop the subject. Here

they were with a beautiful day on their hands, the first really warm, bright day of spring, and he didn't want to waste it worrying. "What are you going to do this afternoon?" he asked abruptly.

"What have you got in mind?"

"How about bumming into town?"

"How about meeting the gang and going to the show?" Bill suggested.

Andy suddenly remembered. "Doggone it, I ought not to go at all. Gram's got a fit of cleaning and asked me to help her with the cellar. I could bum into town and hack around for a couple of hours, but I'll have to be back by four. We could go to the ball field and see if anybody's there."

"Okay. How about leaving now?"

Bill wound up his cleared line, while Andy put his fish in his grandfather's creel and explained that he wouldn't be home for lunch. Gramps was really shocked that he was willing to pass up a dinner of fried trout. Just the same he felt in the pocket of his torn pants and fetched out a crumpled dollar and gave it to Andy.

The boys were in luck, for a neighbor woman happened along on her way to town. She dropped them off at the ball park, down by the river. Some fifth and sixth graders were there and were choosing up sides for a game, and were glad to welcome Andy and his pitching arm.

At first his pitching was a little erratic because he was out of practice, but after three innings his control came back. He didn't try anything fancy, but his fast and slow balls confused the other team, and his side won by a score of 6-2.

He and Bill started thumbing their way home, and were lucky again and hitched another ride with a man who put Andy down at the end of his own lane.

Gram had worked up a good mad, figuring he had forgotten all about the cellar. The kitchen clock chimed four just as he entered. She was scowling and rolling pastry dough. Andy said, "Hey, Gram, you forgot something. You promised you'd help me clean the cellar today. Remember?"

She swung at him but she was laughing, and they had a fine time working together, putting the cellar to rights.

II

THAT SUNDAY Gramps refused to go to church. At ten o'clock Gram sent Ellen out to find him, and Ellen reported that he was sitting on a keg in the barn, rubbing his knees and moaning that his legs weren't strong enough to carry him up the aisle, if he got as far as the church without collapsing.

Gram was looking particularly pretty this morning in her blue suit, having paid a visit to the beauty parlor the day before. Her short, gray hair curled around her face. She sat down suddenly, and Andy saw that she was trembling. "It was nice of Mrs. Otis to offer to take us to church," she said. "It meant a lot to me that we should all go together. I want people to see we're still good, churchgoing folks, even if we are fighting the authorities."

Ellen glanced at Andy, murmuring soothingly, "We'll go with you, Gram." Was Ellen thinking the same thing Andy was, that Gram seemed frail and helpless this morning?

He reluctantly dragged himself up to his room. Dressing for church meant the whole bit, the best suit, white shirt, tie and polished shoes. He was losing the battle with the tie and had decided to let the women cope with it when Gram called up the back stairs, "Andy, don't bother. You're not going. That horrible old man hasn't even started on his chores. You get him off that keg he's sitting on, and make him help you. Come, Ellen, we'll meet Mrs. Otis out on the road."

It took Andy just about thirty seconds to get out of his good suit and pull on a flannel shirt and dungarees. Gramps still sat on the nail keg, his rough, calloused hand playing with Toby's ear. The collie blissfully shut his eyes. "Toby and I are getting awful old," Gramps said. "Your grandmother's too young for me, Andy. I'm tired, trying to keep up with her and her gallivanting. I should have known better than to marry a young woman."

"She's only two years younger than you are, and you've been married to her for forty years," Andy pointed out.

"Yes, I know," Gramps said, "and practically every Sunday in those forty years she's hauled me off to church. If that isn't gallivanting I don't know what it is."

"How did you convince her you had to stay home to do chores?" Andy asked. "I mean, after all, I was the one who burned the papers and buried the garbage, and Ellen fed Toby and the cat. What chores are you talking about?"

"Somebody's got to change the cedar shavings in Toby's sleeping box."

"I did that last week."

14

"How about the hen house, then?"

"That needs doing," Andy conceded.

"That's what I told your Grandma," Gramps cried triumphantly. "I told her I couldn't go to church and sit at ease in my pew, enjoying the sermon, knowing those poor hens were roosting in such a dirty house."

Andy roared with laughter, and seized the hoe and marched outside. He yelled "Shoo!" at the hens, and banged on the roof to drive them out. Then he scraped the floor with the hoe and pulled the manure into a pile for Gram's flowerbeds. He marched back to the barn and grabbed a square bale of hay, loosened it and filled the boxes so the hens could lay their eggs on fresh hay.

He glanced at his watch. Gramps glanced at his too. "Humph!" he said. "You're a fast worker."

"It took me just seven minutes to do the job you persuaded Gram would take you all morning," Andy told him. "Come on, Gramps. What was your real reason for staying home?"

For one of the few times in his life, his grandfather sounded very serious. "I planned something I can only do with you, son," he said quietly. "I want to walk the land with you."

Andy was surprised, for they had walked the land together many, many times. He had the sense to say, "Okay," without arguing, for he realized that the old man had some good reason.

Gramps took his gnarled walking stick from a nail by the barn door, and they set out. They started at the eastern boundary, the corner of a stone wall on the

town road, where their land adjoined that belonging to Ivor Grabowski, their Polish neighbor. Keeping close to the wall they edged the swamp land. The ground was wet from spring rains, and in places Andy had to help his grandfather jump from hummock to hummock.

He hoped the old man would rest when they reached higher ground, but Gramps charged straight up the hill, pushing through a blackberry thicket. They were on the slope of Mount Tom.

They turned to look, as they always did, in this place shaded by white birches, carpeted with ground pine. The land fell away to the south with a clear view of hills and more hills, shimmering blue in the spring sun.

Andy felt peaceful, the way he often felt when they climbed the hill. He loved the mountain so much, he sometimes felt as though he owned it. Nobody knew why it was called Mount Tom, and sometimes in his private thoughts Andy renamed it Andy's Mountain.

Gramps rested a moment and caught his breath, then went on. At the next wall they swung west and soon came to the spring lot. Gramps had remembered to bring a brush along. Andy lifted off the square stone that covered the spring. Clear, pure water bubbled out of the earth, and a pipe carried it a quarter mile down the hill to the house. Several times a year they had to climb the hill to clean the strainer, which kept leaves and bugs out of the pipe. Andy took off the strainer, and Gramps brushed it clean. Andy replaced it and put back the stone. Then they resumed their walk.

They circled their slope of the mountain and here reached the highest ground. At last Gramps was willing to rest. They sat on a clump of rocks. The morning was very still, the only sound the whine of Grabowski's tractor, which made a noise like a giant bee. "Mr. Grabowski's rushing the season," Andy commented. "It's too wet to plow."

Gramps didn't hear. He cleared his throat, then said quietly, "I planned on taking this walk someday with your father, Andrew. Life worked out differently, though. My son is gone, but you're here, and you'll inherit. Of course you and Ellen will inherit equally, but you're the man. You'll have to look

17

after your sister and also your Gram, as long as she lives."

Andy knew this, had always known it. Why had Gramps brought him up the mountain to tell him again today?

"Everything that lies before us from here belongs to me and your grandmother, and will someday be yours and Ellen's," Gramps went on. His voice had a sound of steel in it. "I want to dispel in your mind forever any notion it won't come to you intact. People may think it's a joke, my fighting the state, but it's no joke. I'm dead serious."

He pointed with his cane. "You can see where the road's coming, cutting a swath through Grabowski's bottom land. They'll soon be working there. Grabowski was glad to sell, for it was poor land they took, and he needed the money.

"From there they want to lay four lanes of road through our best land and right through our house. If we gave in and sold they'd come with their wrecking crew and bulldozers and tear down everything. I don't care about the barns, they're old and ramshackle and are ready to come down. But those men would level our home and burn it, and they'd fill the cellar hole and it would be gone."

Gramps turned to Andy and his blue eyes were opaque and gray. "Son, they're not going to do it," he said. "You're too young, so I'm not seeking your help to fight alongside of me. I'm just telling you, this property will come to you and Ellen intact, and your grandmother will finish out her days in her own

18

home. That road will come onto our land only over my dead body."

"Gramps!" Andy cried. "Please, Gramps, don't ever say a thing like that."

As he watched, the twinkle came back into his grandfather's eyes, and Gramps' lips twisted in a grin. "I scared you, didn't I?" he said. "I meant to, sonny. I just want you to realize that I mean what I say. Now we'll go back. Gram's fixing a pot roast for dinner, and we'll surprise her. We'll cook the dinner and when our gals come home from church they'll sit down at the table like a couple of real ladies."

That was the end of serious talk for that day. The chill that was laid on Andy's spirit refused to go away, though.

Gram tried to open up the subject while they were eating dinner. She mentioned that the minister planned to make a call, that he wanted to discuss with Gramps his battle with the state. Gramps answered that the minister was welcome to call but that he'd better mind his own business, which was running the church, and not stick his nose into what didn't concern him.

Monday came with showers, a typical April day. At seven-thirty Ellen and Andy were waiting in their shelter for the school bus, when Bill Otis joined them. The bus rumbled up. Bill and Andy sat together, while Ellen found a seat with Roseann Grabowski, her best girl friend.

The road problem was uppermost in Andy's mind. "I've got to talk to your dad," he told Bill. "I mean, I

19

really want to consult him as a lawyer. Do you think I should go to his office, or would it be better to come over to your house tonight?"

"I don't know," Bill said. "Why don't you call him and ask?"

Their bus was one of the early ones, and they had a half hour to wait before school began. The principal gave Andy permission to use the telephone in his office.

Andy caught Bill's father at home, before he left for work. Mr. Otis must have realized that the appointment was a serious matter, for he suggested that both boys come to his office after school. He would drive them home when he finished his work.

The bus let them out on Main Street, in town, that afternoon. Andy had never visited the law offices, upstairs over the Amestown Savings Bank, and he was impressed. Three secretaries were working at desks, and one said, "If you'll sit down and wait, gentlemen, I'll tell Mr. Otis you're here."

Andy fidgeted in a leather chair, growing more and more nervous. "Gee," he muttered, "I've got an awful nerve to come here and bother your father when he's so busy. I mean, I can't pay him or anything like that."

"Forget it," Bill said grandly, with a wave of his hand. "Dad wouldn't let a friend of mine pay, anyway."

He got up too, ready to take part in the conference, when the secretary told Andy he could go in. His father stopped him, ordering, "Wait outside, Bill. I'll see Andy alone."

20

Andy didn't know how to begin, once he found himself seated in front of the big desk, but Mr. Otis made it easy. "I've got a fair idea of all that's happened, but you go ahead and give me your version, Andy," he suggested. He took notes, leading Andy along.

Andy told how the affair had started the previous spring, a year ago. His grandfather had received the first letter from the State Highway Department, requesting him to sell a portion of his land for a right-of-way for the new road. Gramps had torn up that letter without answering it. A few weeks later two men had arrived, and stated that they were ap-

praisers for the state, sent to find out how much the land was worth. Gramps had ordered them off his doorstep, and shouted at them until they got into their car and drove away.

"Did he threaten them?" Mr. Otis asked.

Andy thought a moment. "I can't remember. He's threatened so many people, I suppose he did."

The lawyer grinned. "Your grandfather is quite a character," he said.

"You can say that again!"

"So what happened next?"

"Well, as I remember we had some peace for a while last summer," Andy said. "Then another man came. I was home, so I heard him. He was nice and polite, and he said he was from the real estate section of the Highway Department and said he was ready to offer a big lot of money for the land, and to reimburse Gramps for the loss of his house and barns. Gramps just yelled at him, 'Get off my property and don't show your monkey face here again!' "

"He's prepared to fight the whole state," the lawyer mused.

"He sure is," Andy said fervently. "He's ready to fight the Army and Navy too, if somebody sends them.

"After that, in September or October, last fall anyway, a letter came and it was registered. Gram signed for it when the mailman brought it, and Gramps was awful mad at her for doing it. That was what they called the notice of condemnation. I don't know what that means."

"It means the State was telling your grandfather

they were seizing the property. They have the legal right to do that, if the public good is going to be benefited," Mr. Otis explained. "If the state couldn't condemn property, we couldn't have any roads, Andy. Nowadays this country needs big superhighways to handle all the traffic."

"I'm not the one you have to convince," Andy pointed out. "Gramps is the one."

"All right, so what did he do with the notice of condemnation?"

"He tore that up, too. He did the same thing when the sheriff showed up at our place. Sheriff Holmes is an old pal of Gramps', but Gramps hasn't spoken to him since that day he came to the house. Mr. Holmes handed him a piece of paper and Gramps shoved it back at him, and Mr. Holmes tried to tell him he had to take it and if he didn't obey it he would be arrested. The sheriff was almost as mad as Gramps was, and when he got in his car he yelled, 'I'll see you in jail yet, George Wheeler!' "

"What he probably brought was the notice for your grandfather to appear at a hearing," Mr. Otis explained. "The state holds a hearing, to listen to the facts on why the land has to be condemned. The landowner is ordered to be there. But of course Gramps didn't go."

"No, he didn't go."

"At that hearing, the price of the land was set by law. The state was prepared to pay the fair market price. Has the sheriff been back since?"

"Yes, he came again. That was about two months

ago. He had a state trooper with him. They had another paper that time, too."

"They brought the order of ejectment."

"I don't know about that. Gram tried to get hold of it but Gramps tore it up in tiny pieces and threw them in the sheriff's face. Mr. Otis, is it true that the police can come and put Gram and Gramps right off their property?"

"Yes, son, that's true," the lawyer said. "I know it sounds like a terrible thing, but it can and does happen when people refuse to accept the fact that the public good comes before their own private good. That's the case here. I've tried to explain all this to your grandfather, tried to persuade him to give in. Saturday, down by the brook, I tried again. He thanked me and told me to mind my own business.

"I can't do that, Andy," Mr. Otis said. "I'm fond of your grandparents, and I hate to see them hurt. It's very, very late in the day for a lawyer to help them much. After all, the road has almost reached their line. I was glad when you asked to see me today, because I wanted to ask you if you thought it would help if I talked to your grandmother. Does she have much influence over her husband?"

"Yes," Andy said. "Gramps is just crazy about her. He'll grumble, and then he'll usually end up by doing what she says. But she can't budge him in this, Mr. Otis. Believe me, she's talked herself blue in the face. Every time they have a go at it, they both get so mad they don't speak to each other for a couple of days. It's terrible."

24

The lawyer stood up. "It doesn't look very hopeful, but I'll see what I can do," he said. "I have one suggestion, though. I'm through here at the office — you were my last appointment. I'll drive you home and outline my idea on the way."

III

THE LAWYER'S IDEA was so obvious, Andy wondered why he and Gram and Ellen had never seriously considered it. Mr. Otis suggested that they start right away looking for a house they liked, in another part of town. "That would give you something interesting to think about," he said. "What's more important, it might give your grandfather a way out. You know, Andy, his trouble may be that he's painted himself into a corner. His pride won't let him back down. If he realized that there's an alternative, it might be easier for him to give in."

"Ours is a big house for Gram to take care of," Andy mentioned. "Ten rooms, that's too many. I remember her saying once that she wasn't as young as she used to be, and wished she had a smaller house."

"A new one that's easier to care for," the lawyer agreed.

"Maybe she's like my mom," Bill put in. "Mom likes to move. She's crazy about the place where we live now, but if Dad said we had to move again, I bet she'd jump at the chance."

His father chuckled and agreed. "Maybe some

women like variety," he suggested. "They don't become attached to houses and to property, as men do."

He stopped to let Andy out. Andy thanked him, and told him he intended to have a talk with his grandmother that very evening.

It didn't work out that way. For reasons known only to himself, Gramps decided that the family was going out to eat. It was five o'clock when he decided this, and Gram had started to fix supper. "We're going on a bender," Gramps announced. "We'll have dinner at the restaurant, and we might even take in a movie afterward."

They stared at him, puzzled. "Why do you want to do a thing like that?" Gram demanded. "I thought you'd turned into a regular stick-in-the-mud, George, and hated to eat away from home. And I'm making your favorite, corned beef hash and fried potatoes."

"You can save it for tomorrow night. You and Ellen, go put on your glad rags."

"How will we get there?" Ellen asked. "Walk?"

"No, Miss Smartie, I'll call the man who runs the town taxi."

"But that costs a lot of money," Gram protested.

"Who cares?" Gramps demanded. "We're not going to live forever. We might as well have some fun."

They said no more. The taxi came and took them to town, and Gramps escorted them into the hotel dining room. He seemed gay and carefree, and told them to order what they liked, not looking at the price. The women chose roast duck, and Gramps ordered a steak and advised Andy to do the same.

"What's gotten into him?" Ellen whispered to Gram, while Gramps was busy giving the order.

"I don't know, but we might as well make the most of it," Gram whispered back.

They held court while they were waiting for their dinner. Andy had always known that his grandfather was thought of as a town character, and that everybody liked him. Gram's name had been Ames before she married; she had belonged to the family for whom Amestown was named. She had served for twenty years on the school board, and was now president of the Historical Society, so she was popular, too.

People came over to the table to speak to her and to congratulate her husband. Maybe they secretly wondered why Gramps was defying the authorities, but they seemed to admire him for it. The men clapped him on the back and said, "Keep up the good work, George," and Gramps beamed.

The dinner was delicious, and there was a lot of it, but Gramps insisted they all have dessert. Afterward they wandered up the street to the movie house.

The picture was a very funny comedy and made them forget their troubles. Gramps' laughter rang out louder than anybody else's. Andy glanced at him and wondered, How can he be so lighthearted?

Andy remembered now something that had happened last fall, when some state officials had come to the farm. Gramps had ordered them off the place. One of them had shouted back, as he was leaving, "Mr. Wheeler, you're nothing but a senile old man!" Was that what ailed his grandfather, Andy wondered. Was he just too old to understand what was happening to them?

Andy shook off the problem and went back to enjoying the show.

He got his chance to talk to Gram the following afternoon. Ellen didn't come home after school because she had a Girl Scout meeting in town. Gram and Toby were at the end of the lane when the bus lumbered to a stop. "How come?" Andy asked. "Did you come to meet me?"

"No, not really," Gram said. "I guess I have a bad dose of spring fever. I couldn't stay in the house; I just wanted to smell the air and see how the trees are leafing out."

They started slowly along, not hurrying Toby, whose legs were getting feeble. Andy brought up the idea of looking at houses in town.

Gram thoughtfully listened. "This isn't exactly a new idea to me," she said.

"You mean you'd be willing to do it?"

Gram looked at him in astonishment. "Sometimes I marvel at the stupidity of the male sex," she said. "Andy, I should think you'd know I'd jump at the chance. Do you think your grandmother is the village idiot or something? Of course I want a new house! I want a small one, all on one floor, with lots of closets. It would have a modern kitchen, and a nice cellar, and tight, warm floors.

"Andy, you don't know much about women," she went on. "I'm so tired of that great ark of a farmhouse, with its crooked walls and wide floorboards,

I could die. Some of those windows have been stuck closed for years . . ."

"Why didn't you say so when the state first started this action?" Andy broke in.

She pulled a shoot of new grass and chewed it, thinking that over. "Because I couldn't join the people who are breaking your grandfather's heart," she said. "I couldn't let him lump me in with his enemies. I have to stay strictly neutral, Andy."

"Gram, that doesn't make sense," Andy said. "If Gramps would only give in and move to town his troubles would all be over."

"Of course it doesn't make sense," Gram agreed. "What you and Mr. Otis and everybody else fail to see is that your grandfather can't be sensible in this matter. Nobody except me knows how much the place means to him. He inherited the house and the home lots from his father, but the rest he put together by buying a few acres at a time. His dream was to hand it all on to our son as a working farm. He built up the herd the same way, a few cows at a time."

Gram paused. "Your father died, and your mother, whom we loved like a daughter," she said quietly. "Gramps didn't lose his dream, though. He was helped through that hard time by the knowledge that he could hand on the farm to you and Ellen. He had to give up active farming and sell the herd, but he put the money aside so that when you grew up you could restock the place. It comforts him to know that the value of the land increases each year, that he can pass on to you a valuable legacy."

Andy had vaguely known all this. He waited for Gram to continue, but she didn't. Finally he asked, "You think he can win his fight?"

"No," she said. "I knew the battle was lost the first day the surveyors came."

"But you're going to stand by him, regardless?"

"That's right," she said. "Regardless."

"Then there's no point in looking for a house so we'd have a place to go when they put us off the farm."

"I've thought about that while we've been talking," Gram said. "Yes, let's go ahead. We'll see Ben Simms, who's the best real estate dealer in town. We'll swear him to secrecy and find out what places are available."

That night Andy slipped out of the house unnoticed. He wanted to see how much distance the highway had made that day. He walked along Mount Tom Road and then across Grabowski's land, to the edge of the ugly swath cut by the machines. He was startled by a red glow near a stone wall, and then Mr. Grabowski called to him, and he realized that the glow came from the farmer's pipe. "It doesn't look as though they got much done today," he commented.

"They didn't work," Mr. Grabowski said. "They found out that my bottom land is softer than they thought, so they'll have to bring in loads of stone for fill. After that they'll have to truck in earth to build up a ramp across the lowest part, to raise the level of the road. The boss told me the whole job may hold them up for two or three weeks."

They exchanged good nights and Andy ran home, feeling more cheerful than he had felt for a long time. The family was getting a reprieve. Maybe, Andy thought, they would have time to gather their wits together and make some intelligent plans before the next crisis came along.

After the roadbed crossed Grabowski's lowland, only one large field lay ahead before the machines crossed Mount Tom Road and reached the Wheelers' property. When they arrived at that boundary, the showdown would come.

IV

SOMETHING HAPPENED TO ANDY at that time that was so important it pushed his worries right out of his mind.

He had always liked baseball, and had started out early in life with a Little League team. He played every chance that came along. The Saturday afternoon he and Bill Otis bummed to town and played at the town ball park had whetted his appetite for more.

Bill too was interested in improving his skills, and came over to the Wheeler place every afternoon to play catch and practice batting. The more they played the more they improved. Bill really startled Andy once by remarking, "You're a great pitcher."

Andy thought he was kidding and gave him a funny look. "No, I mean it," Bill said. "I wouldn't say it just to make you feel good. When we lived in the city my dad took me to a lot of big league games. Boy, I've missed that since we moved up here! I know what I'm talking about. You have a great fast ball, and you have good control."

Andy laughed off Bill's compliments, but he suspected that what Bill said was true. He was no bragger, and he would have died rather than admit he thought he was pretty good. The fact was, though, that when he stood on the mound he felt like king of the hill. He could tell his pitching arm what to do and it did it. He could put the ball over the plate at the speed he chose, at the right height between the batter's shoulders and knees.

The sixth grade had a fair-to-middling team this year, and there was no question about who pitched; it was always Andy. They had no uniforms, because the school system only provided those for the junior high and senior high teams. The boys bought their own blue caps and brought their own balls and gloves and bats.

They had no coach, either. Mr. Mott, the math teacher who coached the junior high team, sometimes stopped to watch when the sixth grade was practicing after school. He gave them a few pointers, and that was all the help they got.

Classes ended at three, and the big yellow buses lined up in the circular driveway. The boys who stayed late to play ball had to get themselves home as best they could, but this was no problem for Bill and Andy. They walked to Mr. Otis' office and hooked rides with him.

One afternoon the team was straggling out the back door of the school, crossing the parking lot. Mr. Mott was standing with Mr. Halsey, watching the boys come out. Somebody asked, "What's he doing here?" Buck Halsey was the director of athletics for the high school, and he was a big shot, revered by everyone because when he was young he had played in the major leagues.

This day they were lucky enough to have two full teams. Eighteen kids had arranged to stay after school in order to practice. They chose up sides, and Andy threw some warm-up pitches to Butsy Graham. Butsy was the only one of the gang who owned a real catcher's mitt. "Okay, let's play ball," Butsy called after a while.

Andy was feeling his oats, enjoying a really good day, and he struck out the first two batters. The third one managed to connect, and hit a long fly ball which landed far out beyond the right fielder and counted as a home run. The fourth batter swung at every ball Andy threw and missed them all.

Andy joined his team on the bench, waiting their turns at bat. Butsy leaned across a couple of other kids to say, "Buck Halsey is sitting in his car watching you pitch. Did you see him?"

Andy shook his head.

Playing ball without an umpire behind home plate always resulted in a lot of arguments. Naturally, no batter would admit that any ball thrown at him was a strike. Joe Silvani went up to bat, and complained loudly and bitterly about a bad call on the part of the other team's catcher. The gang was converging on Joe and the catcher when the men walked onto the field. "Come on, kids, break it up," Mr. Halsey ordered. "Mr. Mott will umpire at home plate for a while."

Things went smoother for the rest of that inning.

Andy's team got a man on base, but couldn't bring him in. The score was still 1-0 when Andy walked out to the mound again. Mr. Halsey followed and stood behind him.

Andy grew more and more nervous. A couple of his pitches were too low, but he managed to put some fast ones over the plate and tricked the batters into swinging at them. Those players went down one, two, three.

He was walking back to the bench when Mr. Mott signaled him. He joined the two men. "Andy, you have a good arm but you're not getting the most out of your windup," Mr. Halsey said. He showed how it should be done. Then he studied the way Andy's fingers held the ball, but found no fault with it. "Keep it up, son," he advised. "I've not said this to many youngsters, but you're a natural-born ball player. You might go a long way. I'll be glad when

36

you get to high school. We can use you." He clapped Andy on the back, and then he and Mr. Mott left.

The gang crowded around to ask what they had talked about, and Andy only said, "Mr. Halsey gave me some pointers." He was walking on air, though. For the rest of the game his arm obeyed him perfectly and as a result the opposing team didn't get a man on base. Andy's crowd got a man on base on balls, and the batter who followed hit a double and brought them both in. The game ended 1-2.

Nobody on the other team acted sore about losing, and some even congratulated Andy on his pitching. It occurred to him that maybe they liked him. He had never thought about his own popularity. This gave him a very warm feeling; it seemed to him that everything was coming up roses for him today.

He and Bill climbed the bank and crossed the railroad tracks and walked up Bridge Street, to find Mr. Otis' car. "Andy, you pitched a really great game," Bill said.

Before, Andy would have just grunted and made light of such a compliment. Today he said simply, "Thanks, Bill." He knew deep down in his heart that what Buck Halsey had told him was the truth.

He was quiet on the way home, for he was thinking deeply. He had always taken it for granted that he would have the kind of a life Gramps wanted for him. When he got older he would go away to college and learn modern agriculture. Then he would come home and build up the herd, and run the place as a dairy farm again.

Of course that was all changed now. The state planned to take the best land right away from the Wheelers. What would be left was mostly swamp and hillside, of little value for farming. This prospect had made Andy deeply unhappy for over a year.

He was sitting in back, scarcely hearing the conversation between Bill and his father, absorbed with a new idea. Had he ever really wanted to be a farmer? He wasn't sure. He was positive of one thing now, though. If a career in baseball was possible for him he would work his arm off and work his heart out to achieve it.

The family noticed that he was preoccupied at dinner, and Gram asked what was the matter; he said, "Nothing."

He thought and thought about his life during the next few days. It seemed as though Buck Halsey had opened a door on a bright and shining future. He waited for a chance to come about naturally, to tell Gramps about all this.

Gramps mentioned that he wanted a few hours of Andy's time on Saturday morning, to lay up the walls that had slipped loose during the winter. Andy asked Bill to help them. Bill planned to come at nine. He was a foot taller than Andy, and heavier, and he was flattered that his strength was needed.

There was a lot of wall to do, and by the time breakfast was over Gramps was itching to get at it. He was in high spirits, happy that spring had come. "Let's start on the west line," he suggested. "Your pal Bill will find us there."

He and Andy began at the road end, one on each side of the wall, laying back the rocks that had been loosened by the winter's freezes and thaws. It was hard work, bending and lifting and wedging the rocks back in place. Gramps was very strong for a man his age; there was still a lot of muscle in his reedy arms. Just the same, Andy worried about him.

They reached a maple tree, having covered a hundred yards, and Andy suggested, "Let's take five. Bill will be along soon." Gramps was willing to lean against the tree and catch his breath.

Here the ground was cleared; the wall edged some of the Wheelers' best fields. Gramps contentedly looked over his land. How often had he made the remark he made now? "Andy, this will all be yours someday."

It gave Andy just the opening he had been looking for. "Gramps, I've wanted to talk to you," he said. "I wanted to ask you something. Would it be a terrible disappointment to you if I changed my mind about being a farmer?"

The way Gramps looked at him he seemed to see Andy not as a thoughtless boy but as a man. He didn't fly off the handle. "What did you have in mind?" he asked.

"I've got reason to think I might be a ball player," Andy said. "Maybe that sounds crazy." He went on to tell how he felt about the game, and how Buck Halsey had encouraged him.

"This Buck Halsey," Gramps said, when he finished, "is he the one who played on a Dodgers' farm team and came up to play in the majors for a few years?"

Astonished, Andy agreed. "That's right. How did you know that?"

"I remember him," Gramps said. "Several years ago, when the Dodgers were still in Brooklyn, I used to watch them on television. Maybe you won't believe it but your Gram was a real fan, too. One summer we even went all the way to Brooklyn, to see them play at Ebbets Field. They had a center fielder named Halsey, and as I remember he was playing ball to earn the money to put himself through college. Every time I've heard the name I've wondered if it was the same chap who lives here in Amestown now.

"Andy, if Buck Halsey says you've got natural ability, he's probably right," Gramps went on. "Those bums were a great team. Maybe Halsey wasn't famous, like some of them, but he had to be mighty good, to play with them."

Gramps chuckled. "I even remember his batting average, how's that for a memory? He left the team before they moved to Los Angeles. His last year he batted .297."

Andy pressed his point home. "If Mr. Halsey's right, what would you think about my going out for big league ball?"

"How about college?"

"I could do what Mr. Halsey did. He had to be a college graduate to get a good job as athletic director."

"What about the farm?"

Andy saw no sense in pointing out that there wasn't any future for the farm. Why ruin Gramps' morning? "It wouldn't do any great harm if I put that off for a few years, would it?" he asked. "I mean, the land would still be here, and most ball players have to quit the game while they're still young, before their legs get tired and their arms give out."

Gramps nodded. "That sounds reasonable." Then he banged his hands together. "Hey, wouldn't that be something if your Gram and your sister and I could sit in a ball park and watch you out there pitching and winning? What does your grandmother say about this?"

"I haven't told her. I wanted to talk to you first."

Bill Otis' head popped up on the other side of the wall. "How come you two are sitting around loafing?"

"We were just chewing the fat," Gramps told him. "You and Andy can work together and I'll keep up with both of you. We'll really make the old rocks fly!"

He spoke the truth. At the end of an hour both boys were puffing and grunting like porpoises, but he still seemed fresh as a daisy.

They were all wearing heavy gloves for protection. Andy kept a sharp watch as he settled the stones in the wall, for snakes hibernated there and the warm sun might bring them out. He didn't mind black snakes but copperheads were something else again. The previous spring one of the neighbors had lost a pet dog when it was bitten by a copperhead.

Sweat ran down Andy's back; his flannel shirt was hot. He was relieved that after a couple of hours Gramps decided to call it a day and finish the job the following Saturday.

For a week the countryside had been silent; the road machines stood where they had been abandoned by their crews. It was an easy week for the Wheelers; the ominous noise of the road machines didn't remind them of their problems. Andy said thoughtfully to Ellen, one afternoon when they got off the bus, "We're like a bunch of ostriches, hiding our heads in the sand."

"Shhh!" she said, putting her finger to her lips. "Oh dear, they're at it again. Hear them?"

They left their school books in the shelter and crossed the fields to the torn area that marked the end of the construction. Huge trucks carrying fill were grinding through the mud, jockeying clumsily to turn and dump their loads. Andy told Ellen what Mr. Grabowski had said, that it would take several days to truck in enough stone and gravel to fill the marshy area and raise the road level. "So, we get a reprieve," he said.

"It's like the condemned man hoping to hear the governor is going to pardon him," Ellen said. "Only the governor of this state couldn't care less. He doesn't know we're alive."

Andy glanced at her, surprised. This was something new he had to contend with, the fact that Ellen wasn't just a stupid little kid. She was a real person, with original thoughts and ideas. "No, the governor

42

isn't going to send Gramps any pardon and let us go on living here," Ellen said. "Andy, I'm scared that the road will just roll right over us if we don't do something soon."

"Do you know whether Gram has talked to Mr. Simms?"

"I don't think she has," Ellen said. "She'd take us with her if she was going to look at new houses. I'll ask her when she's planning to do it."

"Talk to her tonight," Andy urged. "We've had a nice, easy week, but I bet it's not going to stay peaceful around here much longer. We've dawdled long enough."

"Maybe we've dawdled too long," Ellen agreed.

She was right. Their quiet interlude ended with a bang. They were at supper when a knock sounded at the door.

Ellen stood up, looking frightened. "Keep your places," Gram ordered. "I'll see who it is."

Gramps was out of his chair too, and heading for the door. His wife caught the back of his shirt. "Sit down," she told him. "I'll handle it."

He paid no attention but kept on going. Gram got to the door ahead of him. Andy and Ellen followed.

Sheriff Holmes stood on the back step, two Amestown policemen in uniform backing him up. The sheriff was middle-aged, but just the same Gramps shouted, "You young whippersnapper, what do you want this time?"

Sheriff Holmes stuck out a piece of paper. Gramps reached for it but Gram snatched it out of his hand.

"What is it?" she asked. "Don't give us any legal folderol, Charlie Holmes. Tell us straight out."

"It's the order of eviction," the sheriff said, sounding miserable. "Emily, you know I don't like to serve any such paper on you and George, but I have no choice. The court ordered me to and I have to do my job."

Andy glanced at Ellen, for a sob had escaped her, and tears were running down her face. That was too much for Sheriff Holmes, who had known her since she was a baby. He bent down and tried to put his arms around her, murmuring, "Now, now, dearie, I'm sorry."

Her head snapped up and she glared into the kindly face and yelled, "You nasty man!"

The situation was getting out of hand. Andy said the first thing that popped into his head, "What's an order of eviction?"

Les Shack, one of the town cops, took it upon himself to answer, "That means you have to get out. You have to vacate the premises in four weeks."

At that Gramps let out a roar like an enraged bull. Andy seized his arm, for he thought his grandfather was about to hurl himself upon Les Shack. Gramps struggled to escape Andy's hold. "What do you mean, bringing a dimwit like that along to do your dirty work?" he demanded of the sheriff. "He isn't even dry behind the ears and he has the everlasting gall to stand on my step and tell me he's going to put me out of my house? Get him out of here, Charlie Holmes! Take him and that other young fool

44

away before I blast the three of you off my doorstep!"

He swung around. The rifle, which was kept loaded with spread shot to use on poisonous snakes, hung on two hooks in the back entry, over some coats. Was it loaded? Andy couldn't remember. He followed his grandfather and found him fumbling for the gun. A winter jacket fell over his head, and then a rain slicker. He bellowed, trying to fight them off.

Andy had all he could do to keep from laughing. He heard Gram say, "You've done your job, Charlie, so you'd better go." By the time Andy had succeeded in untangling Gramps from the coats, the car was heading down the lane.

V

LOSING HER TEMPER upset Ellen badly. Gram had quite a time with her, trying to quiet her down, for she couldn't stop crying. Soon she complained of a headache, and after that she began to throw up, and Gram took her upstairs and tucked her into bed.

Gramps too was very upset, seeing his beloved granddaughter sick, and forgot his rage against the officers of the law. Really subdued, he retired to the living room with his evening paper.

Andy helped his grandmother clear the table, and wiped the dishes as she handed them to him. "Something has to be done right away," she told him. "We can't waste any more time. I'll talk to Ben Simms tomorrow."

It seemed to Andy that an air of doom hung over the place the next day. Everyone was thoughtful and quiet at breakfast. Andy looked around the comfortable kitchen, wondering, Is it true that a month from now we'll be out of here? He just couldn't imagine it. It seemed like a bad dream, a nightmare, that this house could be torn down and burned, or whatever the wreckers did, and then leveled.

He had a lump in his throat he couldn't swallow. Ellen was acting strangely. When they walked down the lane to meet the school bus her face was blank, expressionless. Suddenly she swerved and walked straight into a tree. She bumped her forehead so hard she fell back, and Andy caught her. "What's the matter with you?" he asked.

"Nothing. I was just thinking."

"Don't do it," he suggested. "Any thinking you and I do won't help. What's going to happen will happen. We'll see how Gram makes out today."

He had planned to stay after school to play baseball, but while he was sitting in class, staring at a math problem on the blackboard, he changed his mind. At noon he went to the office and called his grandmother to tell her he would come home on the bus with Ellen.

It was lucky he did. A light rain was falling, when they reached their lane. "Maybe Gramps didn't come out to get the mail," Ellen said. There weren't any letters in the box, but the mailman had left the Kingston *Bugle*.

Most people in the area took the *Bugle*. Kingston was the nearest city that had a daily paper, and the *Bugle* printed sections of local news for all the towns around. The Amestown section was usually in the back, but today something on the front page caught Ellen's eye. "Look!" she cried.

The picture was taken from the road, showing the lane and the house and outbuildings at the end of it, and the hills beyond. "Wheeler Homestead in Ames-

48

town Doomed," the caption said, and underneath, in small print, "See story, page 10." Ellen's hands shook so, the paper rattled. Andy took it from her and turned the pages and read the story aloud.

"Despite the family's long battle to save it, the house belonging to George Wheeler, on Mount Tom Road in Amestown, will soon be torn down. The old, colonial farmhouse is a landmark in the area, and has sheltered the family for six generations. Mr. George Wheeler, aged 73, has sworn that the new Route 73 will not cross his land. This correspondent understands that Mr. Wheeler has stated it will be done 'only over his dead body.'

"Such threats of course have been made many times in many places, but seldom has the juggernaut of the State Highway Department been swerved from its course. The new superhighway, planned to relieve traffic congestion in the western part of the state and to speed traffic to the north, is an integral link in the federal and state system of roads.

"According to local authorities, the Wheeler land was condemned several months ago. Mr. Wheeler was notified of the hearing but failed to appear. As recently as last evening the indomitable old man was still refusing to acknowledge the eviction order, which was served on him by the proper law enforcement officers.

"Amestown residents express admiration for Mr. Wheeler's determination, and sympathy for him and his family, which consists of his wife, Mrs. Emily Wheeler, president of the Amestown Historical Society, and his grandchildren, Andrew and Ellen. Few, however, feel that the family has any real prospect of winning the case."

Andy refolded the paper and started slowly on. His sister suddenly snatched it out of his hand. "We can't let Gramps see it," she said. "We'll have to hide it or burn it up."

"He'll have to see it. He's going to want his crossword puzzle. You know what would happen if we fibbed and said the paper wasn't delivered. Gramps would call the post office and blast them."

"I suppose so," she said. "Just the same, this is going to upset him something awful."

"Why will it?" Andy asked.

"Well, seeing it in print like that makes the whole thing so much more real."

They quietly entered the kitchen, and Andy was hoping to find Gram alone, but she wasn't there. The room was fragrant with the aroma of fresh coffee, and their grandfather sat at the table, a steaming cup before him. "Where's Gram?" Ellen asked.

"She's gone," he announced. "That's what happens when a man marries a young woman, she goes off gallivanting, leaving her family to shift for itself. She went to a country auction with her pal Ruth Brooks. There are cookies in the jar for you, and there's milk in the icebox. Get yourselves something to eat, and give me my paper."

Ellen held on to it. "Gramps, promise you won't be upset if you read something," she begged.

"Read what?" he demanded. "That the country's going to the dogs? That's not news, granddaughter. Give me the paper."

He spread it before him, cleaned his glasses with a corner of the red-checked tablecloth, and put them on. His eyes widened. Without comment he turned to page ten.

Ellen poured milk for herself and Andy, and they watched the old man anxiously. They needn't have worried. Gramps' eyes were twinkling when he looked up. "What do you know?" he said. "We're famous! Look at that, young 'uns, there are your names, right there in the paper spelled out proper and all. And the newspaper even got in what I've always promised, that the consarned road will only cross our property over my dead body."

They stared at him. Ellen tried to put her question carefully. "Gramps, don't you mind what it says?"

"Mind? Why should I mind? It's the truth, isn't it? I mean, that all our neighbors and friends wish us well and are urging us on?"

This wasn't the truth. Maybe people wished them well but few of them were urging Gramps on in his disastrous quarrel. "That wasn't what Ellen meant," Andy said. "She meant where it says that nobody ever wins in a fight with the state."

"Oh, that."

"Yes, that," Andy said. He saw that the newspaper story might be a means to persuade the old man. "Gramps, now that you see it in black and white you can look at it the way other people do. Can't you change your mind? Don't you think we ought to buy a house somewhere else? That's what Gram wants . . ."

His voice trailed off, for Gramps wasn't listening. He was reading the piece again. "This story's all right," he said. "They couldn't come right out and say the state is wrong and the law ought to be on our side, but you can see they feel that way. What's that they call me, 'the indomitable old man?' Your grandma's going to be mighty proud to learn that's what she's married to, an indomitable old man."

"Gramps, you're hopeless," Ellen told him severely.

The minute Gram came in the door Gramps pushed the paper in her face, ordering, "Read that."

"Oh, my," she murmured, when she saw the picture. "Oh dear," she said, when she turned to page ten. "I ought to resign," was her first comment.

They didn't understand what she meant. "I ought to resign as president of the historical society," she explained. "The society's important in the town. The president ought not to be involved in a scandal."

Gramps rose straight out of his chair. "Bah!" he shouted. "Bah and humbug. They'll be proud. We're fighting for our rights, and that's historical. We're making history, woman! If those folks in the society don't see it that way then they're just a bunch of weak-kneed ninnies. What do they think the American Revolution was all about?"

"This isn't the American Revolution and you're not General George Washington, you're just a pigheaded old fool!" Gram shouted back.

After that they pointedly ignored each other, and

52

it was a very uncomfortable evening for the children. They all went to bed early. When Gram and Gramps were shut in their room, though, Andy could hear them murmuring together. Once Gramps' voice rose, "Woman, are you with me or against me?" But at least they were speaking.

Gram managed to have a few words alone with Andy before breakfast the next morning. "I've talked with Ben Simms and he wants to show us a house today," she told him. "Nell Grabowski is taking me into town to meet him, and we'll pick up you and Ellen after school. I don't like doing this behind your grandfather's back, but it's the only way."

The two were waiting in the parking lot when Ellen and Andy came out. Mr. Simms drove north, out of town, and swung between stone gates where a sign hung, "Valley View."

"Gram, this is a housing development. You know how Gramps feels about housing developments," Ellen mentioned.

"Yes, I know, but let's wait until we see the house," Gram suggested.

The hardtop road wound along, bordered by neat, clapboard houses, set on tiny lawns. Woods fringed the development. They reached the end of the hardtop and a dirt road advanced among tall trees. They came to another clearing, and Mr. Simms explained that here the houses were to be built on two-acre lots, that they would be very nice homes.

"Very nice and probably quite expensive," Gram commented.

It occurred to Andy that the Wheelers could afford a nice house, with the big, fat sum the state had offered for their land.

Only one house in this new section was finished. Mr. Simms parked in the driveway. Bricks made a winding path around a lamp post to the front door.

Andy noticed that the women wore identical expressions of wonder and delight as they stepped inside. A tiny entrance hall opened into a living room, where a picture window framed a view of thin woods, leafing out now in the early spring. A brook ran along the bottom of the slope. "That's a feeder brook of the West Tom River," Mr. Simms said, answering Andy's questions.

Gram and Ellen left the men, seeming to forget their existence, lost in the pleasure of exploring. Andy heard them opening doors, heard Ellen say, "Closets and closets and closets."

"Yes, and such beautiful big ones," Gram murmured.

"Oh Gram, what a marvelous kitchen!"

"Yes, it would be child's play to cook here."

"Two bathrooms."

"Yes."

"Both tiled."

"This would be your room, and the next Andy's. Gramps and I would take the one across the hall, with the yellow bathroom."

The real estate agent let them discover the house by themselves. Andy trailed after Gram and Ellen, keeping within the sound of their voices. He understood how they felt. If he was looking for something to criticize he would have a hard time finding it, he realized. Compared to this, the farmhouse was an awkward, shambling ark, and no matter how hard Gram struggled to keep it clean, she fought a losing battle. And Gram wasn't getting any younger, Andy thought with a pang.

She and Ellen came on him when they returned to the kitchen. He was studying the automatic dishwasher; the house had every device to make work easy. "Oh Andy, we forgot you," Gram said, giving him sort of a dazed look. "What do you think?"

"I think it's just great."

"You do? You really do?"

"Gram deserves a break, too," Ellen said, her jaw setting stubbornly, as though she expected Andy to give her an argument. "All we think about is what Gramps wants. She's got rights too. She ought not to have to work so hard."

"Oh, I don't look at it that way at all," Gram protested. "What we want most is for your grandfather to be happy." She added softly, "But I do like this little house."

Nobody spoke on the ride home. Mr. Simms didn't say a word, and must have known he didn't have to. The house had sold itself.

VI

WHEN THEY REACHED Dog Leg Corner Gram asked
Mr. Simms to let them out, and promised she would
call him soon. They strolled home slowly, deep in
thought. Ellen broke the silence. "When are we going to show the house to Gramps?"

"We'll have to pick just the right moment to tell
him," Gram said. "We can't spring it on him without warning."

"Why do we always have to think about his feelings?" Ellen sounded rebellious.

"I told you, dear. Because we want him to be
happy. Because we all love him," Gram said. "He's
a wonderful man. Don't be fooled, children, because
he jokes and roars and threatens. He's very frightened, and his heart is breaking. I honestly don't
know what will happen to him when we take him
away from the farm and put him down in a new
place.

"We three know that's how this business is going
to turn out," Gram added. "Nothing can stop it.
How he will act when that time comes, and how we
will handle it, that I can't imagine."

Andy said nothing, agreeing with his grandmother completely. He knew, as she did, as Ellen apparently didn't, what the land meant to Gramps.

Before they left the house in Valley View Mr. Simms had pointed out to them the boundaries of the two acres, making it sound as though two acres was a tremendous lot of land. Andy had realized that even if his grandfather dragged his feet, he could walk such a skimpy little piece of land in ten minutes.

How many times since he came to live at the farm, after his parents died, had he and Gramps walked the Wheeler land? It took a good two hours, if they didn't hurry and followed the walls and fences, tracing the boundaries exactly. And every square foot of it was precious to his grandfather. Worse than that, Valley View had no Mount Tom; the developers couldn't crowd a mountain onto a few tiny acres. Gramps loved Mount Tom as much as Andy did. Probably Gramps thought of it as his, just as Andy thought of it as his own mountain.

Old Toby came slouching to meet the three, and Gramps was waiting at the back door. "Where have you been?" he asked.

He didn't wait for an explanation, but started to accuse Gram of hiding something. Drawers were pulled out and cupboards were ransacked, and the kitchen was a mess. "Where's the paper Charlie Holmes served on me?" he demanded.

"I hid it where you won't find it," Gram told him. "My lawyer told me you have no right to tear up legal papers."

"Since when have you had a lawyer? Who's this fancy lawyer?"

"It's Mr. Otis, and he's kind enough to want to help us."

"We don't need any help from anybody."

"That's what you think," Gram said. "I say we do!"

For a moment it looked as though the battle of the night before was about to be renewed. Then both the old people mastered their tempers. Gramps grumbled, but he helped his wife tidy the kitchen so she could start to cook supper.

They had forgotten that this was the weekend Boy Scout Troop 2 was coming out from town, to camp overnight on the slope of Mount Tom. Gramps had always allowed the scouts to use his side of the mountain, and he and Andy had cleared the underbrush from a level site near a spring.

Andy's father had built a log cabin there, when he was a boy. The roof had fallen in, but the log sides were intact. The Amestown Boy Scouts had made it their project to give the cabin a new roof and floor.

This wasn't Andy's gang; but he knew many of the boys who piled out of cars on Saturday morning. The backyard was a bedlam for a while. The sensible mothers were obviously relieved to get rid of their offspring for two days, but the less sensible ones looked anxious and tearful. Gram came out to assure them that the boys would have a fine time and nothing would happen to them.

Gramps loved the excitement, and helped the frantic scout master sort out the boys and their loads of blanket rolls, food and equipment.

The scoutmaster was new at his job, and asked Andy to come along and show them the trail. They set off. Andy was holding the barbed wire, helping the boys through the first fence, when he heard his grandfather bellowing from the yard. He couldn't hear what Gramps said, so he nodded his head anyway, agreeing.

The chattering boys, loaded with equipment, crossed the meadows and struggled through the swamp, jumping from tuft to tuft. Beyond the brook they reached the orchard and the wooded slope of the mountain. Strips of red flannel tied to trees were supposed to mark the trail, but Andy noticed that many of them were missing. Birds liked to get hold of such strands, to weave the bright threads into their nests. Andy made a mental note to bring along more flannel strips and re-mark the trail the next time he came up.

They reached the campsite, after a half-mile scramble up the hill. When they leaped the brook that tumbled down the slope, Andy saw that it was unusually full and loud. Heavy rains the week before had swollen all the brooks in the area. The spring, fifty yards from the cabin, was choked with soggy leaves.

He realized now what Gramps had been yelling about; he wanted Andy to clear the other spring, the one that fed the house and barn. Gram had complained the night before that the faucets were airbound, and the water pump in the cellar labored as though not enough water was coming through the line. Andy needed the brush to clean the filter. He would have to make another trip up the mountain.

He forgot about water problems and had a good time helping the boys set up tents and make camp. For some it was a first adventure of spending a night in the woods, and they were wildly excited. They seemed like a bunch of amateurs to Andy, and their leader didn't act as though he knew much more than they did. They fell all over themselves getting the tents up, and banged their thumbs driving the tent posts, and when one of them spied a skunk waddling across the clearing several boys took off after it. Andy yelled at them to come back, and it was lucky they obeyed before the skunk got a chance to defend itself.

It was noon when Andy got back to the house. Two of the scouts returned with him, for in the confusion the camp stove had been forgotten. Gramps came out to ask if Andy had cleaned the spring, and Andy admitted he hadn't, because he didn't have the brush with him. Gramps started to get mad. "Why couldn't Ellen do it?" Andy asked. "At least she could have brought me the brush. She had nothing better to do."

"Nothing better is right," Gramps snorted. "Do you know where she and her friend Roseann Grabowski went? They went to a ballet class to learn to dance, that's where. Your grandma and Mrs. Grabowski took 'em. Of all the foolishness I ever heard of!"

"Of all the tomfoolishness!" was the way he greeted

Ellen and Gram, when they arrived home soon after. "I suppose now you know all about ballet dancing, young lady, so let's see you do it. Come on, do us a ballet."

"Stop that, George," his wife ordered sharply. "What's gotten into you?"

Gramps growled that nobody cared about the farm or did any work except him, and his fun-loving grandchildren wouldn't even help out by cleaning the spring. Andy started to argue but a look from his grandmother stopped him. Gramps subsided soon after, realizing he sounded silly.

The two scouts had been standing around, listening. "Why don't you take the stove back up the hill?" Andy asked. They said they couldn't find it.

Everybody searched, but the stove was nowhere to be found. One of the scouts remembered that when the troop had met in town early that morning, the stove had been put in Mrs. Petry's car. Gram telephoned Mrs. Petry but there was no answer. Andy went down cellar to get an old oilstove that was kept for emergencies.

The small, two-burner stove was gummy with oil and dirt, and the wicks had crumbled. Gram got lunch while Gramps cleaned the stove, filled the oil tanks and put in new wicks. The scouts looked so hungry, Gram fed them too.

Gramps was really having a great day, with lots of activity and lots of people to growl at. Three o'clock came before the stove was in working order. "Are you sure you can find your way back up the hill?"

Gramps asked the scouts. They shook their heads. "Andy will take you," he told them. "Ellen, you'd better go too, and do something useful after wasting an entire day learning to dance on the points of your toes."

"It'll be a pleasure," Ellen said with a toss of her head. "Anything would be a pleasure that gets me out of this house."

"The only thing that dancing teacher taught you was to sass your elders and betters," Gramps retorted.

The stove was clumsy and heavy, and the boys were sweating when they reached the camp. "Look out, there's a girl!" rang through the clearing, and boys scattered in all directions. They had taken off their shirts because it was a hot day, but they weren't naked, and Andy guessed they just felt like yelling and running.

He showed the scoutmaster how the stove worked, but he didn't have any real faith the man had the slightest idea how to use it. Then he and Ellen left.

The spring lot was quiet, dim and cool. Andy pulled leaves out of the tiny pool with his hands, then lay on his stomach to brush twigs and other debris away from the strainer. A tin cup hung on a branch nearby, and they both drank.

"I'm not in any great hurry to get home," Ellen said. "Gramps is in such an awful mood, anything can happen. Oh dear, I'll be glad when this is all over and we've moved into the new house. Next week Gram and you and I will have to start packing, whenever we can get Gramps out of the way. It's lucky it's spring vacation week. After that we'll have only two more weeks to get moved and settled."

Andy scowled at her, pretending to be stupid. "What do you mean, only two more weeks after spring vacation?"

"That's when we'll be evicted."

"Don't be a sap," Andy said. "They can't do that."

She swung around, gawking at him. "Are you out of your mind or something?" she demanded. "You know as well as I do, the police will come and put us off the place. And I'll tell you something else. That's okay by me and Gram. We'll all be better off, living near town in that nice house."

"No, we won't!" Andy shouted.

She stared at him for a minute, then said, "You're as bad as Gramps, you're off your rocker too. I'm going home." She marched down the hill, her back stiff, bristling with indignation.

Andy watched her go. He and Ellen had always gotten along well, not in the cat and dog way of most brothers and sisters. Maybe this was because they were orphans. Now, though, all Andy felt for her was dislike. She and Gram were wrong.

He was glad to be left alone, for he wanted to think. Lately his heart had felt like a lump of lead in his chest, because he had meekly given in to the idea that the whole world was right and Gramps was wrong. Now it seemed to him that what Gram had said was probably true. Behind Gramps' bluster there was a badly frightened man.

Andy shredded a tuft of weeds through his fingers, thinking, If we give in and let the wreckers come, Gramps will surely die. I'll tell Ellen that, the next time she opens her yap. How will she feel about that?

The only fault Andy had ever found with his grandparents was the fact that they were old. They had been everything to him, had filled his life after the terrible night they came to take him and Ellen out of their parents' empty house.

He wasn't so worried about Gram; she was frail but there was something indestructible about her. Gramps was different. The loss of his home and his land might destroy him.

Andy's heart felt lighter, for he had made up his mind. Whatever happened, and whether his grandfather was right or wrong, he was going to line up on his grandfather's side.

VII

Gram fixed supper that night on trays, and they carried them into the living room because Gramps wanted to see a movie about World War I. He had served as an officer in that long ago war, which seemed like ancient history to Andy and Ellen. He wolfed his dinner down, not taking his eyes from the screen. "Eat more slowly, George," Gram warned. "You'll get indigestion."

"It wasn't like that at all," he muttered.

"What wasn't?" Ellen asked, and Andy glared at her, hearing the tartness in her tone.

"The trenches in France. They weren't nice and dry and comfortable, the way they look in the movies. Andy, did I ever tell you about Ypres?"

He pronounced it "Wipers." He had told Andy about that battle at least a hundred times, but now Andy answered, "No, I don't think you ever did, Gramps."

Just then a jagged streak of light flashed past the window, the crash of thunder following close. The picture on the TV tube vanished, then reappeared. "Pull the plug, so the lightning won't burn out the

66

set," Gram told Andy. They sat eating in front of the blank screen until Gram said, "We look like a bunch of halfwits. Let's take our supper back to the dining room."

They were all thinking of the campers, and Gramps went to the window, peering into the darkness toward Mount Tom. By a flash of lightning Andy saw the rain scudding across the yard. Wind lashed the maples that sheltered the house. "It ain't a fit night for man nor beast," Gramps said.

"I hope that scout leader has sense enough to bring the boys down," Gram added.

"What will we do if he does?" Ellen asked.

"We'll bed them down somehow."

They finished dinner. Gramps stayed at his post by the window. Finally he said, "Here they come." They saw the gleam of flashlights crossing the fields, and soon heard yelling and laughter.

The scouts poured through the open door into the warm kitchen. Gram hurried to make hot cocoa for them while they dripped puddles on the linoleum and outshouted each other, telling how the tents had collapsed on their heads, and lightning had split a tall tree near the camp.

The scoutmaster looked pale and distraught. "Never again," he muttered:

"What's the matter?" Andy asked, but he couldn't keep the grin off his face.

The man pulled himself together and gratefully accepted a cup of coffee. "Can I use your phone, Mrs. Wheeler?" he asked. "I'll start calling the parents."

"You can use the phone," Gram told him, "but why call folks to come out on a night like this? Our barn's dry. Your boys can bunk down in the hay."

The boys swarmed around their leader, begging him to let them spend the night in the barn. "They ought not to sleep in wet clothes," Gram pointed out.

Pleased with the excitement, Gramps took charge, "You ladies, go in the other room and stay there," he ordered. "You young 'uns, take off your clothes."

He and Andy strung lines, crisscrossing the kitchen, and turned on the stove oven. The boys stripped and hung up their clothes. It was ten o'clock before they were all dressed again, and ready to go out to the barn.

The telephone kept ringing, and Gramps told the anxious mothers to spread the word around that the boys were well and safe. The rain was still coming down in torrents when Andy escorted them out to the barn.

Gramps had collected all their matches, not trusting them in the loft filled with dry hay. Old Toby looked bewildered when the army of scouts invaded his domain. Andy showed them where to bed down, and when he left they were shouting and jumping in the hay, and he doubted that their exhausted leader was going to get any sleep that night.

The women had gone up to bed, and Andy and Gramps put the kitchen to rights. "This farm is still good for something, if it's only to give pleasure to some kids," Gramps said with satisfaction. "Those men in power over at Capitol City, they think it's of no account because it isn't a working farm anymore. They think they can rip it out just because they take a whim to. This place is worth fighting for."

"You're absolutely right," Andy agreed.

Gramps gave him an odd look. "Sonny, I thought you were on the other side," he said. "I thought you'd lined up with your grandmother and everybody else who wants me to give in."

"I'm not lined up with them."

"Are you ready to fight, too?"

"Yes, Gramps, I'm ready to fight, right alongside of you," Andy told him. "Now hadn't we better go up? It's way past bedtime."

This Sunday was a special day. The members of the church took turns inviting the minister and his wife for dinner, and the Wheelers' turn had come around. Gram didn't try to urge Gramps to go with them, when her friend Mrs. Brooks stopped by to take her and Ellen to church. He and Andy had a good excuse for staying home, the fact that they had to look after the place because it was swarming with Boy Scouts.

Andy climbed the hill with the boys, and helped them take down the tents and pack up their equipment. Parents in cars arrived, and soon the crowd was gone.

"Do you know why your grandmother didn't try to make us go to church?" Gramps asked, as he and Andy watched the last car depart. "She wanted a

69

chance to prime the minister. He's going to take me aside and give me a lot of good advice. Stick by me, son. I need my ally today."

The two dressed in their best, to please Gram, and came out to welcome the young minister and his wife. They were new in town; Mr. Nesbitt had taken over the Amestown church only the year before.

Gramps had a bad habit of arguing with ministers, but today he refrained. He carved the roast beef and served the Yorkshire pudding and peas, and when he looked at the minister his eyes twinkled. This made Gram uneasy, and she took a firm hold on the conversation, keeping to the subject of church affairs.

Finally she had to leave the dining room, and Ellen and Mrs. Nesbitt got up too, to clear the table. Gramps had his chance. "Young feller, I suppose you came today all primed with quotations out of the Bible, why I should meekly hand my farm over to the state," he said.

Startled, Mr. Nesbitt denied that. Then he grinned. "As a matter of fact, I don't believe there are any suggestions in the Bible on what to do when the Highway Department wants to build a four-lane highway through a man's land," he said. "Traffic problems weren't so acute, back in Bible times."

Andy laughed, and Gramps leaned over and slapped the minister's shoulder. "You're all right, sir," he said. "As my grandson might put it, you're okay. But I've got a quote for you. You'll find it there in the Bible, 'A man's home is his castle.' "

"I doubt that," Mr. Nesbitt said. "You might find

it in English law. You're not going to draw me into an argument on the rights and wrongs of your case, though, Mr. Wheeler. As far as I can see you're a hundred percent right, and the state is also a hundred percent right, so it's a draw. Just the same, for the life of me I can't see why you can't compromise, sir. If the state only wants a few acres, that still leaves most of your farm intact."

"They want the heart of this place, the good land. They want my barns, and the house that has sheltered the Wheelers for six generations. What's left is worthless, and I'd sell it or even give it away, if they took my best fields."

The minister said gently, "Your wife is deeply worried about what is happening to your family."

Gramps had no ready answer for that, because he adored Gram. While he was trying to think of one she came in and set the apple pie in front of him to be served. There was no more serious discussion.

Gramps happened to mention that Andy showed real promise as a pitcher. The minister's face lit up, and he questioned Andy. He wasn't just trying to be a good sport, he really knew baseball. The ladies withdrew to wash the dishes and listen to a symphony concert on the radio, and the men sat around the table and talked baseball.

Everybody went out to the car when the Nesbitts left. "I want you to come and watch sometime, when my grandson pitches a game," Gramps told the minister.

"I'll do that, and in return I want you to come to

church without your wife dragging you there by the heels," Mr. Nesbitt answered, and they all laughed.

"There's a likely young fellow who will go far," Gramps commented after they were gone.

"I hope he talked some sense into your head," Gram said.

A cloud came over Gramps' face; his cheerful mood was spoiled. He wasn't angry, though. He put his arm around his wife.

Andy turned away, feeling that nobody should watch when married people showed their affection for each other. He heard his grandfather say, "I'm sorry I'm causing you misery, Emily."

"You are, you are," she said, "but I'd still rather be married to a stubborn old fool like you and have the misery, than be married to anybody else."

"I have to hand on this place to you and the children intact, not in bits and pieces, when I die."

"You're not going to die, George, but you're not going to leave the place to Andrew and Ellen intact, either. You have to make up your mind to compromise."

"No, that I won't do."

"The time's getting short," she warned.

"I know," he said somberly.

How short it was getting was brought home to all of them the next day, when work on the road resumed. Andy realized how peaceful life had been while operations were suspended. Now it sounded as though an army of trucks had arrived.

Right after breakfast he and Ellen set out to see

what was going on. Spring vacation for the schools had begun, so they were free.

A massive landfill had been undertaken, to bridge Mr. Grabowski's swamp lots and to raise the level up to the rest of the road. Mr. Grabowski was sitting on his wall, watching. "What are they going to do about Mount Tom Brook?" Andy asked.

The farmer pointed with the stem of his pipe. "You see that tile, down there at the bottom? It had to be made special for the job, it's ten feet in diameter. The brook will flow through it."

"What if we get a flood, like we did a few weeks ago?" Andy asked.

"The engineers figure that tile can handle any rise in the brook."

The three sat watching the trucks dump their loads and turn and go back for more earth. As long as they had known him, Andy and Ellen had been a little afraid of this neighbor, because he was a silent, taciturn individual. Now he chattered pleasantly, and Andy could guess why. The highway that was causing his own family so much grief was a blessing to these people on the next farm.

All their lives Ivor Grabowski and his sons had worked from dawn to dark, but had barely eked out a living from their poor acres. Now they were on Easy Street. The money for their land was like a dream come true. Now they could afford luxuries like Roseann's ballet lessons, and a new truck, and a television set. Now Mr. Grabowski could afford to sit idly for a whole morning watching other men work.

Andy remembered one of his grandmother's sayings, "It's an ill wind that blows nobody good."

Roseann joined them on the wall. Ellen started telling her all about the house in Valley View, about the cunning kitchen and the darling wallpaper in her bedroom and the adorable tiled bathrooms. She sounded like a ninny and while Andy listened he was getting mad. What right did Ellen have to discuss

family business with an outsider? His spirits were
sinking lower and lower.

If the showdown didn't come before, it would
surely come when the landfill was finished and the
road bridged the low ground. Blacktop trucks would
start arriving. Mount Tom Road was at the top of the
slope, and the barbed wire fence and stone wall that
marked Gramps' east line lay just beyond the road.

When that point was reached the bulldozers and earth movers would advance upon Wheeler land.

Andy hadn't been sleeping well lately; he suffered from nightmares. One bad dream kept recurring. In it, the family was sitting around the dining room table when the bulldozers charged straight through the outside wall. He and Gramps and Gram and Ellen ran screaming while the walls and roof collapsed.

That night in the dream Andy and Ellen and Gram escaped, but Gramps was caught, trapped and pinned by heavy beams. The nightmare was so vivid, Andy had to turn on his light to drive it away. He shivered under his cotton blanket, although the night was warm. Was the dream a warning? Did it mean that Gramps would die?

VIII

A DELEGATION ARRIVED at the farm that week. They appeared suddenly; no one heard them coming. The minister stood at the back door with the sheriff and a young man who introduced himself as Steve Jones, a reporter for the Kingston *Bugle*.

Although her husband glowered at her, Gram invited them into the kitchen. The minister hastened to explain, "Sheriff Holmes and I didn't bring Mr. Jones. He happened to come along just as we turned in at your road."

"That's right, I didn't mean to barge in on your little party," the reporter said cheerfully. "I'll take some pictures outside, while you talk. I'd like a few words with you later, Mr. Wheeler."

"Stick around," Gramps ordered. "I'll be glad to talk to you, young feller. We appreciated that nice story your paper printed awhile ago. I may have more to say to you than I do to these two."

The reporter started wandering around, snapping pictures of the house and outbuildings.

"I don't know how a fine man like the minister happens to be in the same company with you, Sheriff,"

Gramps said coldly. "Go ahead, Sheriff. It's your nickel, you're making this call. I didn't ask you to come."

"George, it doesn't look as though you've even started to get ready to move," the sheriff said.

"Who says I'm moving?"

Mr. Holmes turned to Gram. "Emily, haven't you knocked any sense into his head?"

"I've tried but I haven't succeeded," Gram said. "Don't forget, he's a Wheeler, and they've always been noted for their thick skulls."

Ellen laughed. "Kids, why don't you go outside and play?" the sheriff suggested.

"No, they stay," Gramps said. "It's their affair."

"What do you expect to do, Mr. Wheeler?" the minister asked. "You're an intelligent man, so I'm sure you have some sort of plan."

"That sounds funny, in view of the fact my wife just got through telling you that I'm dim-witted," Gramps commented. "That's right, I do have a course of action in mind, sir. It will unfold itself when the right time comes."

There was an uncomfortable pause. It was clear that the men didn't want to start a fight by asking what Gramps' plan was, and it was equally clear that he was dying to be asked. Finally Sheriff Holmes said, "I guess there's a misunderstanding here. The story's going around town that you folks have been looking at a house in that new development, Valley View. We figured you'd be in the midst of packing by now, since the deadline is only a little over two weeks away. The minister wanted to let you know that some of the church folks would like to help you with the hard work, and I came to tell you that a couple of fellows are ready to loan trucks. Your friends would move you free of charge, on whatever day you set."

No one spoke. The sheriff blundered on, "People figure you'll be holding an auction. We know how it is, if you live in a place for a long, long time, you accumulate a lot of stuff you don't need. That's especially true if you're moving out of a big house like this one into a smaller place. I spoke to Ham Metcalf yesterday. He's the best auctioneer in this county . . ."

"You're taking a lot on yourself," Gramps broke in. "You're not only moving me out of my home, you're hiring an auctioneer to sell off my possessions!"

The sheriff went right on. "Ham agrees he can handle the sale, but he needs to know the date, so he can get some signs made and advertise the event in the papers."

"You've run off at the mouth and said a lot, Charlie Holmes, but so far you haven't spoken one word of the truth," Gramps said.

Gram looked unhappy, and scared, too. "Charlie's right about one thing, George. It's true that I went to look at a house in Valley View."

"Oh Gramps, you'll love it!" Ellen exclaimed, taking her grandfather's hand. "It's just perfect, it's the dearest little house."

He shook her hand off. "You took the children?" he asked his wife.

"Yes."

Gramps' eyes bored into Andy's. "You went, and never said a word to me," he accused Andy. "I know how your Grandma feels, and maybe she's justified, according to her lights. Women hate quarrels. Oh, I've known for some time she and Ellen have been packing on the sly. But you, son, you told me you were lined up alongside of me."

"I am!" Andy cried.

"It doesn't sound that way."

"I changed," Andy said. "I saw you were the one who was right."

The minister spoke then. "Mr. Wheeler, I cannot let you do what you're doing, without protest. It's wrong to play on your grandson's love and respect, to get him to join in an action that is illegal and may be dangerous."

Gramps' color was rising. His whole body shook as he raised his arms threateningly. "You two, get out of my house!"

He advanced upon them and they backed out the door. The reporter came running across the yard. "You, come here!" Gramps barked. "I'll give you my statement in front of these two witnesses. Nobody's going to pull down my house because I'll stand in front of it with my shotgun. They'll have to kill me first. Your paper said that before, but now you're hearing it straight from me. Say in your paper you heard it right out of my mouth. Do you hear?"

"Yes, I sure do, and thanks a lot, Mr. Wheeler," the reporter said, and jumped into his car.

The minister hesitated, then started for the house,

but the sheriff caught him back. They too drove off.

"George, that was a terrible way to talk to the minister," Gram began.

Her husband ignored her. "Andrew, if you meant what you said, now's the time to prove it," he said. "You can help me or not, as you please, but you'll have to decide. You'll have to fish, or cut bait and go ashore." He stalked out to the barn.

Andy found him piling tools into his battered tool bag, a hammer and nails and a chisel. He handed Andy a saw. Andy walked beside him, past the barn and across the east meadow. "Gramps," he said.

"No," his grandfather said, "let's not talk, sonny. The time for talk is over."

The gate that for years had kept the herd in the grazing pastures was swung back. Gramps knelt on the damp ground and began hammering at the bolts that held the hinges to the posts. They were rusted, and refused to give. "Let me do that," Andy begged.

"No. Go back to the barn and fetch a can of oil."

The oil, poured over the hinges, made the job easier. Finally the big, heavy gate was laid flat on the grass. They tried lifting it but they could carry it only a few feet before they had to drop it. "Why don't you wait while I get the tractor?" Andy suggested.

"Now, why didn't I think of that?" Gramps said admiringly. His good nature was restored, and the twinkle was back in his blue eyes. "Can you hitch up the trailer?"

"Why not?" Andy said. "I've done it a hundred times."

The tractor was in good working order; Andy saw to that. He loved the machine with a special kind of love, and kept it greased and full of oil and gas. He often went to the barn just for the pleasure of wiping it clean. It took him only a minute to back it through the wide doors, to drag the trailer up and jockey it into place and drop the ball that made the hitch tight.

He and Gramps struggled to lift the gate high and lay it across the trailer. Gramps scrambled in to steady it, and Andy slowly drove across the home lot, carefully avoiding bumps and woodchuck holes. "Where to?" he asked.

"Stop at the barn. I've got a couple of good posts stashed away in there."

They drove down the lane to the main road. Andy dug the post holes where his grandfather indicated,

and set the posts and filled in around them. Gramps then took over.

Andy grew nervous with impatience because the old man was so fussy. When he finished, though, the gate was firm and swung smoothly on its hinges. "Steady as the Rock of Gibraltar," Gramps commented.

He had brought along a padlock. He screwed the hasps in place, put on the lock and snapped it shut. Then he stood back to survey his work. "They won't break that down unless they come with an army tank," he said.

Andy was piling the tools in the trailer when Bill Otis came running along the road, calling, "Hey, wait up!" He climbed aboard and swung his legs from the back of the trailer while Andy drove to the barn.

Toby was running around the yard, making half-hearted attempts to round up Gram's chickens. The stupid birds were remarkably clever at finding any break in the wire of their yard, and a dozen had escaped and were squawking and running. Gram came to the back door, and she looked angry, and also pale and sick. "Tie Toby," she called. "He's only making things worse!"

Andy snapped the collie's chain to his collar, and he and Bill put in a frantic half hour catching hens. Bill was getting his hands badly pecked, until Andy showed him how to catch the runaways from behind so they couldn't swivel their heads around and reach him with their sharp beaks.

Gramps sat on the keg and watched, his hand stroking Toby's head. "We've got to get ourselves another dog," he told Andy, when the boys settled on the ground near him, panting. "Toby's earned his right to an easy old age, and we'll keep him as long as he lives, but we've got to get a younger dog to do some of the chores around here."

"Like what?" Bill asked. "You don't need a cow dog any longer."

"There are other chores, keeping hens in their place, barking when intruders come. Every farm needs a good barking dog."

Bill was only half listening. "Mr. Wheeler, did Andy tell you?" he asked.

"Tell me what?"

"That Mr. Halsey invited him to pitch with the high school team, at a practice session? When's it to be, Andy? I want to go and see how you make out."

"So do I," Gramps said. "Isn't that something, my grandson being singled out for such an honor?"

"It's not such a big deal as all that," Andy protested.

"Yes, it is, and I want to go."

"It's set for tomorrow," Andy admitted. "I didn't plan to let anybody know, because I might not make out so good against a bunch of big guys."

"We'll be there, Bill and I," Gramps announced. "We'll sit in the grandstand and cheer. Modesty's a fine thing, son, but that's carrying it too far, not to let your own family know."

Whenever he had a piece of news, Gramps' first thought was always to tell Gram, and he sought her out. He started to tell her about the honor that had come Andy's way, but she didn't give him a chance. She was ironing in the kitchen, and set the iron down with a thump. "Where were you when those hens got out?" she demanded.

"I was doing a job of work for you," Gramps said. "I was hanging a gate down by the road, so trespassers won't bother you anymore."

"Never mind about a gate. I don't want a gate. Where was that great dog of yours, that Toby? If he's too old to keep the hens in their place, the least he could have done was to bark and let me know."

Gramps was beginning to get mad. "Look, woman, your hens are back behind the wire where they belong, and I've been telling you all winter that we need another dog. I've said we should call the dog warden and ask him to let us know when he picks up a stray that would make a good pet and a good farm dog."

Gram's gray curls trembled as she crashed the iron down on the board. "We don't need more animals, we need less, where we're going," she said. "I've made an arrangement with Mr. Grabowski to buy the chickens, but we'll have to take Toby with us, and I've told Ellen she can keep her cat . . ."

"We're not going anywhere," Gramps broke in. Andy and Bill and Ellen were standing around listening, and he added, "Let's not fight in front of the kids, Emily."

Gram wouldn't stop. She just went on, telling how she had to do all the work around the place and it was too much for her, and if Gramps would just stop acting like he'd lost his wits and fighting the whole world they'd all be better off.

Gramps stood and took it, watching her closely. Finally he said, softly, "Emily, are you sick?"

She backed into a chair and started to cry. "Yes, I'm sick, I'm just a bundle of nerves, I'm worried right out of my mind. My head aches and I can feel a fever coming on, and I don't know where we're going to end up. We're going to be put out on the road with all our belongings and no roof over our heads and all on account of your foolishness, George Wheeler!"

Bill was looking scared and he said, "I guess I'd better be going home," and went.

"Emily, march straight upstairs and get into bed," Gramps ordered. "I'll call the doctor. Ellen, put on the kettle and make your Grandma a nice cup of tea."

Gram showed no willingness to do as she was told. He lifted her and helped her up the stairs. Ellen and Andy could hear her protesting that she didn't need a doctor, all she needed was a husband who would show a little common sense and face facts. "Facts are facts!" they heard her exclaim from the top of the stairs. "Only an idiot refuses to face them."

Ellen made the tea and carried it upstairs. When she came back to the kitchen Andy saw that she was in a temper, for her young face wore the same look as Gram's. "How is she?" Gramps asked.

"I wouldn't be surprised if she was real sick," Ellen said. The children weren't in the habit of defying older people, but she went right on, "Gram has rights, too."

86

"I'm protecting your Gram's rights," her grandfather said.

"No, you're not, you're driving her right out of her mind!" Ellen shouted. She changed her tone. "Gramps, won't you please just go and look at the house and see how nice it is? Andy, tell him."

Andy wavered. He didn't seem to have any mind of his own, these days, he felt so whiffled around. Gramps was right. So were Gram and Ellen. Where did that leave Andy? "It would please Gram if you'd look at the house. You could just go and see it," he mumbled.

The telephone shrilled, interrupting them. Gramps took it off the hook. Being interrupted in the midst of an argument, he forgot to speak politely. "Who's there?" he yelled.

He listened. The children heard him say, "You work for the Associated Press and you want to come and see me? That's mighty nice of you, Mr. Singer. Come anytime, I'm always home. You head north after you leave Kingston. When you get to Amestown, just ask the first person you see where George Wheeler lives. There isn't a soul in this county that can't tell you how to find the Wheeler place."

IX

Nothing was said about baseball the next day. At one o'clock Bill appeared; he and Andy were planning to bum to town.

"Where are you going?" Gramps wanted to know.

"I told you about it, Gramps. I'm going to pitch with the high school team in a practice game," Andy told him.

"I want to go too," Gramps said.

Andy reminded him that the reporter might come to interview him. His grandfather acted like a child trying to decide between two attractive treats. "The reporter feller might or might not come today, and I can't miss watching you pitch," he finally decided. "I'll call the town taxi and we'll go in style."

He was in a wonderful mood as they started out, but he changed as soon as the taxi turned onto Mount Tom Road. Although the fill job across Grabowski's lowland was not yet completed the bulldozers had gone ahead, breaking new ground. A gash of newly turned earth a hundred feet wide reached to Grabowski's last wall. Gramps gasped when he saw how close the machines were to his line. Only the

width of the road separated them from the easterly
boundary. "Stop!" he cried.

He scrambled out of the taxi and across the torn
earth with surprising speed. The area looked like a
battlefield, a no-man's-land that armies had been fighting over. Andy and Bill jumped out and ran after
him. When they caught up he was standing in the
path of a giant earthmover, waving his arms like a
windmill, calling, "Stop, stop!"

The driver, perched high in the air, threw gears
to stop his forward motion and the engine sputtered
and died. His face was like a thundercloud, and Andy
guessed he was angry because he had come so close

to running Gramps down. He jumped to the ground, shouting, "Don't play games like that with me, Grandpa!"

Gramps stuck his face right into the driver's. "Don't call me Grandpa! Who are you? You're not a local boy, that's sure. No local boy would be so stupid as to come this close to my land!"

"You're right I don't live in this hick town," the man told him. "I don't know anything about your land, mister, or who you are. I work for a construction company from Kingston and the boss laid out the job I was to do, and I'm doing it, so get out of my way. And don't you ever step in front of a big machine again. The next time the operator might not stand it on its ear to stop in time."

"Where's your boss?" Gramps demanded.

"He's probably in his office. It's a trailer parked in the yard of the next farm down the road."

Andy took the old man's arm to help him over the rough ground. "Gramps, if you want to fight with these men that's okay, but I can't hang around," he said. "I have to be at the ball park."

Gramps nodded. "We'll just stop at Ivor's for a minute."

The taxi turned in their neighbor's yard. Gramps hopped out and banged on the trailer door. "Hey, you in there." The door opened and he stepped inside.

While they waited Andy looked around, and a chill went over him. The Grabowski farmhouse was going to be spared the highway's destruction, and why should it? They probably didn't care too much about their house; they had lived in it only a few years. The place was neat enough, but they hadn't bothered to paint, or to plant shrubs and flowers like Gram's colorful borders. They were so glad to get the money, they wouldn't have minded moving away and finding another farm. Yet the engineers had laid out the road so it saved their house and drove right through the Wheelers'.

Gramps emerged with a satisfied look on his face. "The boss has his orders," he said. "He'll make sure the machines stop at our line. I told him if he touches our wall or our barbed wire I'll have the law on him so fast he won't know what hit him."

The taxi driver delivered them at the ball park. Some of the high school gang was warming up on the field, while others were gathered around Mr. Halsey and Mr. Mott. Gramps told Andy, "I'll keep out of your way," and scrambled over the seats and planted himself in the bleachers.

Andy slowly approached the bench. He had sense enough to realize that these big boys would resent him. That was natural. How else would high school guys feel about a younger kid being asked to join them? Mr. Mott introduced him, "Fellows, this is Andy Wheeler." They said, "Hi, Andy," and he said, "Hi," and there was an awkward pause. The most horrible feeling came over Andy that he was going to make a complete fool of himself.

The second varsity squad took the field. The plan was for Andy to play with them, pitching against the regular high school team. The first team's pitcher was sitting on the bench, and Andy realized he would probably never have a more critical observer. He walked out to the mound, all the boys watching, and it seemed like the longest walk of his life.

How many times had he seen on television a pitcher taking that walk out to the mound, in a major league game? Hundreds of times. He had always wondered what the man was thinking. The pitcher's responsibility was really a terrible thing; the rest of the team was important but he was the king pin. It had always seemed to Andy that the mound of a baseball diamond must be the loneliest spot on the face of the earth, and now he found this was true.

He had tucked a handkerchief in his hip pocket. He wiped his sweating hands. "Ready, Andy?" the catcher called.

"As ready as I'll ever be, I guess," Andy croaked. The catcher tossed the ball.

They tried some warm-up pitches. Then the batter stepped to the plate. Andy was used to pitching to smaller boys, and his first three balls were low. He tried to cure that on the fourth pitch, and it went wide and high. The first batter was on with a walk.

None of the boys said anything — they were trying to be kind because he was only a little kid — so they didn't even glance at each other, to let their looks show what they thought. They didn't have to. Andy knew they were all wondering, What did Mr. Mott and Buck Halsey see in this little squirt that they thought was so great?

Mr. Mott was umpiring behind home plate, and he walked out while the second hitter swung his bat over his head, limbering his arms. "Take it easy, son," Mr. Mott advised. "We've got all day, so take your time."

Andy just nodded. There was no point in making excuses for his poor showing. Excuses never did a pitcher any good, on a sandlot with Little Leaguers or in a major league game. Either a pitcher had the stuff or he didn't, it was that simple. He wiped his hands on his pants, scooped up some dirt and dusted the ball with it, and wound up to pitch to his second batter.

Bill Otis had once offered the opinion that Andy had as good control of a fast ball as he did of a slow one, and remembering that, Andy let go with a real blast. It was still a little low but it was higher than the batter's knees. The boy swung and fanned air and a surprised look came over his face. Mr. Mott sang out with the most beautiful word in the English language, "Strike!"

The next two went wide of the plate. The fourth was another fast ball delivered at waist level. "Strike!" Mr. Mott called again. "Two balls and two strikes." Andy changed his style and pitched a change-up, a soft curve. "Three strikes," Mr. Mott called. "One out."

The next boy who came to the plate managed to connect with Andy's slow ball, and Andy turned to see what happened. He was so used to playing with sixth graders he didn't really expect anybody in the outfield to catch the fly ball, but the centerfielder reached up and picked it out of the air.

Andy's heart rose. Two men were out. The first batter was still dancing around off first base, taking longer and longer leads. Andy quick-pitched to the first baseman, but the runner made it back to the bag in time.

Andy's confidence was returning, and he steadied down. He deliberately put out of his mind that today was a very important occasion for him, and concentrated on delivering the ball where he wanted it. The situation was difficult because he and the catcher had no signals arranged, so the catcher couldn't tell him what kind of balls to throw. He used his own judgment and got the third man out, and the runner was left high and dry on first base.

Nobody said anything when he joined the team on the bench. The two coaches didn't speak to him. It was as though they were deliberately leaving it up to him, to sink or to swim. Luckily he was so far down on the batting order he didn't have to come to bat to show whether he could hit. The first three men on his team went down in order, and that was the end of the first inning.

Andy walked out to the mound, and glanced up at the bleachers while he waited for the catcher to return a practice throw. Gramps didn't wave or anything, to distract his attention. He seemed to know how desperately Andy needed to concentrate. Bill was grinning from ear to ear, and stuck up two fingers in a V sign for victory.

94

There wasn't any yelling on the field, kidding and talking it up to encourage each other. It was the most silent game Andy had ever played. He kept his mind strictly on the job at hand, to make his arm obey and deliver the ball where he wanted it, at the speed he chose.

The tension built up as the game went on. When Andy came to bat in the second inning he struck out, and in the fifth he hit a long, fly ball which a varsity fielder easily caught. It was clear that Andy was no great shakes as a hitter, but that didn't matter today. What Andy had going for him today was a shutout.

After that first inning, when the batter reached first, only two more men got on base. One made it to third, but the junior varsity catcher picked him off at home plate when he tried to beat out a long throw. The other was left on base, to wither on the vine when his teammates struck out.

The game went into the eighth inning still tied up 0-0. Andy was hoping and praying somebody on his team would get a run, to give him a safety cushion. His arm was tiring and he didn't know how much longer he would have his stuff.

That was what happened. The boy who went to the plate just ahead of Andy in the batting lineup hit a home run. It sailed over the left fielder's head and hit the grass, rolled across the road and came to rest in a clump of bushes.

Andy went out to pitch the ninth inning with that run for insurance, so his work was easier. He threw carefully, taking plenty of time to dry his hands and wind up. The three batters who faced him went down in order. The game was over.

Although the day was cool Andy was dripping with sweat, from nervousness. He slowly walked to the bench. He felt awkward and clumsy again. Wasn't anybody going to say anything?

The boy who had caught for him broke the ice. "Nice work, Andy."

A senior varsity kid joined in, "That's some fast ball you've got, Andy."

The captain of the senior high team came over. "Show us how you throw that slider, will you, Andy?"

Bill stood beside him, his face wreathed in a wide smile. Mr. Mott and Mr. Halsey watched while Andy earnestly explained his theory of how to pitch a slider.

He didn't want to hang around, he wanted to get away. Bill had arranged for his father to pick them up after the game, and Mr. Otis was waiting. "Come on, Gramps, let's go," Andy ordered abruptly. They walked to the car, and most of the team followed, talking baseball. The ice was really broken. They had accepted Andy.

What would have happened if he hadn't had his stuff today? They would have rejected him. Kids who were serious about baseball made a coldly critical audience, and that was right.

"How did it go?" Mr. Otis asked.

"It went okay," Andy said modestly.

Gramps had kept his enthusiasm bottled up just about as long as he could, and now it burst out. He really poured on the praise, comparing Andy with all the great pitchers of the past forty years. Andy finally had to stop him. "Come off it, Gramps," he scoffed.

His grandfather grinned sheepishly, and subsided.

X

WHEN GRAM HEARD about Andy's successful afternoon she hugged him. "It's about time something nice happened to this family," she said. "We can stand a bit of good news."

Not so Ellen. She was so completely ignorant on the subject of baseball, she couldn't understand her grandparents' enthusiasm. That night when Gramps started in all over again describing the beautiful balls Andy had thrown, she looked annoyed.

She was wiping the dishes for her grandmother. She finished and hung up her towel and said, "Come on, Gram, let's finish packing that stuff in the cellar while we've got Andy to help lift the boxes."

She added, "Of course we don't want him to get his great pitching arm all tired out, but it wouldn't hurt him to help a little with the moving. We've only got a few more days."

"I'm tired, dear. That can wait until morning," Gram protested. Andy saw that she didn't want to spoil her husband's happy evening.

Gramps didn't miss the point, though. How could he? Packing boxes had been appearing lately all over the house. "Miss Know-It-All!" he exploded. "Who do you think you are, trying to boss the rest of us? Let me tell you, young miss, I'm still the boss around here, and what I say goes, and that goes for you too."

"The child's only trying to be helpful," Gram told him.

His evening was ruined, though. He grumbled an apology to Ellen, then glowered at all of them while they worked around him, bringing up full boxes from the cellar and filling empty ones with the contents of the kitchen cupboards. His face got sourer and sourer and finally he said, "You might leave Andy and me a few pots and pans and dishes, Emily. That is, if you can spare some you won't need at that wonderful house you're moving to."

"Meaning what, George?" Gram asked.

"Meaning you can desert the ship because you think it's sinking, but Andy and I are staying."

Gram sank into a chair and wiped her face with her apron. "Oh George, when will you begin to face the facts?" she moaned.

"You're the one who's running, gal. I'm the one who's staying and facing the fact that nobody is going to turn me off my land." Gramps stood up, assuming he had said the last word and silenced the opposition, and stalked upstairs.

Andy finished piling the heavy boxes in a corner. "It looked for a while there as though we were going to have a nice evening," he said gloomily.

"Your sister was wrong tonight," Gram said. "Ellen, I've tried to tell you, you can catch more flies with honey than you ever can with vinegar. Please leave your grandfather to me."

"Excuse me for saying so, Gram, but I don't notice that your methods are working too well," Ellen answered. She too apparently thought she had said the last word, and departed.

Andy and his grandmother were left alone. "Words, words, words," she murmured. "Andy, I'm so sick of arguing I could scream. Let's us go to bed too."

Andy puttered around the yard the next morning, wiping down his beloved tractor. He was taking off the distributor head to clean the points when he heard the phone ring. There was an extension in the barn, and Gramps rushed to answer.

He ran out of the barn. "Andy, hop to it and unlock the gate," he ordered. "The Associated Press feller called from town, and he's on his way up here."

"What's so great about this AP feller?" Andy inquired.

"He's going to tell our story in all the big city newspapers."

"What's so great about that, Gramps? You sound like a publicity hound, as though you want to see your name in the papers."

Gramps huffed and puffed, then calmed down. "I only want him to tell our story so the Highway Department will stop those machines. So they'll be shamed into taking an alternate route and leaving us alone. Be sure to padlock the gate up tight, after you

100

let him through. We don't want Charlie Holmes or the police sneaking in after him."

Andy swung open the gate for a yellow convertible with two people in it. A girl moved over to let him in, after he had locked the gate. The driver introduced himself as Dick Singer and the girl as Connie Conway, who had come along to take pictures. "I see you have this place set up like an armed camp," he observed.

Andy longed to warn him that the right kind of a story might help the Wheelers, while the wrong kind could only hurt them, but he didn't know how to do it. "My granddad's kind of a nut on the subject," was the best he could do.

"So I gathered, but he sounds like an interesting man."

Andy thought that over, and agreed, "You can say that again."

He had forgotten that this was the day for Ellen's ballet lesson and Gram's shopping. He was relieved to see them getting into Mrs. Grabowski's car. This interview would go a lot easier without Gram contradicting her husband and Ellen making sharp remarks.

Gramps waited inside the house until the women were gone. He had slicked down his white hair and put on a jacket. He had evidently thought out how he wanted to conduct the interview. He shook hands with Mr. Singer and greeted Miss Conway in a courtly way. Then with a dramatic sweep of his arm he said, "This is the old Wheeler homestead. It's a landmark in this part of the country and the state plans to destroy it and mash it as flat as a matchbox. I want you to see it."

They had to tag after him all over the house, up to the attic to see the heavy beams, like the framework of an old ship, down the front staircase with its graceful half-circle, through every room. He pointed out the fireplaces, the wide oak boards in the floors, the ancient green panes in the windows. He explained how he had been born in the sunny front room, like his father and his father's father before him. He showed the Dutch oven, and the small cupboard over the living room fireplace where his ancestors had stored their gunpowder to keep it dry. "There's history here," he explained. "That's what they plan to wipe out, living history."

He's really hamming it up, Andy realized. These folks are from the city. What do they care about our family history?

Miss Conway, though, was obviously impressed. "It's beautiful," she said. "You're right, Mr. Wheeler, it's a lovely house. I don't wonder you're upset to think of its being destroyed."

"It won't be destroyed if you and this young man do your job well."

Mr. Singer looked alarmed. "You can't hold us responsible," he protested. "What I write may not have the slightest effect."

"I think it will," Gramps said confidently. "Let me show you."

He led them into Andy's bedroom, which had a

northerly view. "I'll show you first where the road can't go," he explained. "That's Mount Tom up there, and it has a total rise of two hundred and seventy-five feet. I don't hardly expect the state to hack out a road over it, or around its flanks. There it sits, blocking the way. Now follow me."

He led them into his and Gram's room, and scowled at the sight of a mound of boxes and suitcases. Gram had been packing her clothes and personal belongings. He went to the window. "There's where the road ought to go, can go and will go, south of Mount Tom Road," he announced. "Those ignorant engineers and surveyors made their original mistake laying it across my neighbor Grabowski's land. They could have saved thousands of dollars of the taxpayers' money if they'd changed the angle to the south before they reached that point. But from where they are now they can alter course."

"Where would it come out again on its original direction?" Mr. Singer asked.

"Down at the crossroads, at Dog Leg Corner. It's out of sight from here."

"How much distance would that add?"

"A quarter mile, more or less."

The reporter was silent for a moment. "I didn't come to argue with you, Mr. Wheeler," he said finally. "You're an intelligent man though, and I'm sure you understand that the Highway Department's job is to lay out a safe, smooth road that takes the shortest distance between the points it's supposed to connect."

"Who's side are you on?" Gramps demanded.

"I'm not on any side. I'm just saying that that's progress."

Andy hoped his grandfather wouldn't explode. That word was like the fuse on a bomb. Now the red crept up into Gramps' white hair. He made an effort, though, and controlled his temper. "If by progress you mean that fools can get somewhere a few seconds quicker, you may be right," he said stiffly. "They rush along the highways at sixty miles an hour, thoughtless and unheeding of the beauty of the scenery, to cut a few seconds off their journey. Why? What's at the end that's so important? But that's progress. Oh my, yes sirree, that's progress!"

Miss Conway tried to help. "You can't push back the clock, Mr. Wheeler," she said gently.

"No, miss, I don't aim to push it back," Gramps told her. "But I sure enough aim to stop it."

Andy was relieved that the two realized they were getting nowhere. The photographer had her pictures and the reporter had his story, and they prepared to leave.

Mr. Singer got behind the wheel. "Just one more question, Mr. Wheeler," he said. "The showdown comes in less than two weeks, isn't that right? What are your plans?"

"You came through my gate," Gramps reminded him. "That's the only entrance to this property, so that's the way they'll have to come. I'll be sitting there with my rifle across my lap. My grandson will be with me. He's a true Wheeler, he won't cut and

104

run. They're not going to shoot down an old man and his grandson, are they?"

Mr. Singer swung toward the barn to make his turn. Gramps wiped his eyes with his sleeve; tears came easily to him these days. Miss Conway was waving good-bye when Gramps called, "Wait, wait!"

"I forgot to tell you something," he said, leaning on the car door. "How could I forget such an important thing? This week my grandson pitched a shutout. What do you think of that? Mr. Buck Halsey, who used to play for the Brooklyn Dodgers, says my grandson is a great natural ball player. You'd better make note of the name, Andrew Wheeler, because you'll be hearing it in years to come. I'm only telling you because this is part of our family history too, and ought to go into the story."

Mr. Singer smiled. "Congratulations, Andy. I'll see what I can do. Good-bye!" The car bumped down the lane.

Gramps and Andy listened to it humming along the country road to town. "They're nice folks," Gramps said. "They have some wrong notions about progress but they're nice folks. They understand."

It was getting along toward noon, so Gramps reheated the breakfast coffee and Andy scrounged around in the pantry and found a bag of sugar buns Gram had been hiding. They sat down companionably at the table. "You and I will have a fine time keeping house together, after our ladies leave," Gramps promised.

Gram found them that way, huddled over their feast. Gramps had commented, watching her and Ellen getting out of Mrs. Grabowski's car, "Don't be surprised, sonny, if this afternoon your grandma and I have the greatest fight in the course of our happy, married life."

He inquired after Ellen's pirouettes and entrechats, two words he had picked out of Ellen's chatter about ballet. Then he poured his wife a cup of coffee and pushed the milk pitcher near her. "Why thank you, George," she said, pleased. "I'll just sit a moment and then I'll start dinner."

"I see you're leaving me," her husband stated.

"What do you mean by that silly remark, George?"

"I noticed up in our bedroom that you're packing your clothes. When a wife packs her duds, that's a sure sign she's leaving her husband."

Gram paled, seeing that a major argument lay ahead, but she didn't back down and try to appease him. "I'm packing all our clothes, except what we'll need in the next two weeks," she said.

He picked up a kitchen chair and turned it over. Andy was startled to see a paper pasted on the reverse side of the seat with the single word, "KEEP." "Do you reckon I'm blind?" Gramps asked. "I've noticed that you've marked various pieces of furniture all over the house. What happens to what you don't mark?"

"They go under the auctioneer's hammer," Gram said. "I'm sorry it has to be this way, George, that I have to make these decisions. If you weren't behaving like a crazy man these days, we'd be choosing together what will go into the new house where we're moving. It breaks my heart to part with our belongings but we can't stuff the contents of this big ark into six rooms.

"If you'd been acting rational these past weeks, we would have gone together to choose a house," she went on. "As it was, the children and I had to do it, but we had you in mind. There's a lovely big yard, and a fine place for your workshop . . ."

Gramps stood up. He was seldom rude to Gram, but now he stalked right out of the house. Gram seldom lost her temper, but now she did. "You stubborn old man, come back here and wait for your dinner!" she yelled.

He just kept on going. Andy went outside and watched him cross the north lot and disappear over the rise. After a while the sturdy figure of the old man appeared, climbing the path to an enormous boulder that a glacier had left on the hillside, thousands of years ago.

Tears stung Andy's eyes. How many times had Gramps led him up there, to sit on that boulder? It was their favorite spot. Many, many times Gramps had contentedly surveyed the peaceful scene spread below and said, "A man may not have a cent in his pants or an extra shirt to his back, but he's a rich man if he can look at a pretty sight like that."

Andy was squeezing between the bars of the gate when Gram called, "You, Andy, come back and eat

your dinner!" He waved and went on, for he didn't want his grandfather to be alone today.

He was picking his way across Mount Tom Brook when an idea hit him that was so brilliant he stopped dead in his tracks. He almost lost his footing on the mossy stones. It was so simple! Why hadn't anybody thought of it?

Why couldn't Gramps stay on his own land? Why couldn't the state seize the acres it needed? That still left the north fields, the swamp, the brook and the mountain. It might be worthless for farming, but it was mighty pretty land. Why couldn't the state make a road and move the house to the very spot where lonesome old Gramps was sitting now?

Andy retraced his steps and ran through the yard. Toby heard him and got up from his sunny spot by the barn door. Andy gave him a pat in passing and ran on.

Gram heard him and called, "Where are you going?"

"I've got to see my lawyer," Andy called back.

XI

It was sheer luck that he found Mr. Otis at home. Mrs. Otis ushered him into the lawyer's study, announcing, "Here's a client of yours."

"Take a chair," Mr. Otis invited. "What's new, Andy?"

"Nothing much, except that I have an idea." Andy went on to outline his plan.

He watched the lawyer's face, hoping it would light up as though Andy had handed him a brilliant solution to the whole problem. It didn't; Bill's father just looked thoughtful. "I've never had any dealings with the state in cases of this type," he said. "I don't know whether they'd be willing to build a road and move a house. How long would the road have to be?"

"Maybe a quarter of a mile," Andy told him.

"That's a lot of road."

"It wouldn't have to be hardtop. They could hack out some sort of a lane, taking off of Mount Tom Road after it's made a dead end road. It would only have to cross the north lots and the brook."

"It would involve building a bridge."

"I hadn't thought of that," Andy admitted. "Maybe that would cost a pile of money, even for a little wooden bridge. And it couldn't be too small if they were going to move the house across it."

"Suppose I get in touch with the highway commissioner as soon as possible," the lawyer suggested. "I won't try to argue the case over the telephone, though. I'll go to the capital."

"That's putting you to a lot of trouble," Andy said.

"I've wanted to help from the beginning. If your grandfather hadn't frozen me out, refusing to discuss the case, I might have been able to work out a solution long ago," Mr. Otis pointed out. "I'm not really working for him, though, because he hasn't asked me to. I'll represent your grandmother, if she wants me. Suppose I call her."

Andy could tell that Gram was relieved that somebody had come up with an idea. Even across the room he heard her exclaim, "Oh, I'd be so grateful for your help, Mr. Otis!"

Andy stood up and tried to thank him too. "Let that wait until I've accomplished something," the lawyer suggested.

Bill was waiting when Andy came out. "I've been hoping something would happen so you wouldn't have to leave the neighborhood," he said.

They spent an hour tramping the fields, figuring out where they would lay out the road if they were the surveyors. It didn't seem too difficult to them.

They heard the clang of the triangle that hung by the back door. In the olden days, when the place was

111

a working farm, Gram had banged on it to call the hired help at mealtime. It had hung silent for a long time, and the racket startled Andy. "I guess Gram wants me for lunch," Andy said, and broke into a run.

"I suppose the big question is money," he told Bill, when they slowed to climb a gate. "We don't have any idea how much it costs to make a road and move such a large house."

He had a hard time staying asleep that night. He kept waking with a start to find his problem sitting like a ghost at the foot of his bed. There were so many angles to the problem, he couldn't get hold of one, to think it through. The time angle bothered him most; there were so few days left before the police or somebody would come to evict the family. The auctioneer was waiting for them to set a day for the sale. The real estate agent was waiting for Gram to sign the agreement to buy the house in Valley View.

Gram looked tired and harassed on Sunday, and Andy guessed she had put in a sleepless night, too. Only Gramps was full of pep and energy. "What's the matter with you folks?" he demanded. "Here I am, wide-eyed and bushy-tailed, and the rest of you look as though you'd been dragged through a knothole."

Andy hated to go off to school on Monday; he dreaded leaving the farm. The truth was, he was afraid of what might happen during his absence.

He got off the bus at Bill's house on the homeward trip, hoping Mr. Otis might be there. He wasn't, but Bill's mother saw how worried Andy was and suggested he call the office. The lawyer was tied up in a conference and couldn't talk, but his secretary gave Andy the information that her boss had called the highway commissioner's office and made an appointment to see him.

Instead of going across lots, he and Bill walked home along the road. Gramps was at the gate. "What have you been up to?" he asked.

Everyone had agreed that he shouldn't be told of the new plan until something happened. They didn't want him to get his hopes up, only to have them dashed. Andy dreaded his questions, but Gramps had something else on his mind. "I'm waiting for Harned Brooks," he explained. "Do you know something? We're famous. Yep, we really are. Harned called to tell me that his daughter saw a New York paper this morning, and we're in it, pictures and all. Harned's bringing me a copy.

" 'Embattled farmers,' that's what they call us, Andy. That's what you and I are, a couple of embattled farmers. Now that folks all over the country can read about us, maybe Charlie Holmes and his police will think twice before they throw us off our land!

"That's another reason Harned called," Gramps went on. "He says he has little to do these days, and plenty of time to watch the road. He'll keep his eye peeled and when he sees the police pass his place he'll telephone to warn us. That'll give us time to get to the gate, Andy. We'll be here to stop 'em when they arrive."

Bill's sharp eyes had noted the rifle leaning against an elm tree near the wall. Andy had already seen it, and also a kitchen chair laid on its side in the tall weeds. "Do you think you can hold them off with your blunderbuss, Mr. Wheeler?" Bill asked.

"That's no blunderbuss, that's a rifle, and it's in good working order, young feller."

"Is it loaded?"

"Sure it's loaded. Wouldn't I look like a fool, facing a hostile mob with an empty gun?"

"Gramps, it will never come to that," Andy said firmly.

"It may, it may, and if it does we'll be prepared."

That Tuesday the hours dragged. Andy sat in class but his mind was miles away. Ellen had the same trouble, and when Andy ran into her in the hall on their way to the lunchroom she was crying. Roseann Grabowski was trying to comfort her. Their teacher had scolded Ellen in front of the class because she had called her name three times before Ellen heard her.

Andy's teacher too had given him a bawling out for inattention, but she knew more about the Wheelers' troubles than Ellen's teacher did. She apologized, and said she guessed Andy had just about all the problems he could manage.

Baseball practice was scheduled for that afternoon, but Andy didn't stay. Ellen begged him to come home. "You're the only man in the family," she said. "Gram needs you."

Andy tried to tell her that Gramps was still head of the family. "No," Ellen said, and her face looked tired and old. "The way he's acting, people are beginning to think he doesn't have all his buttons."

114

A pain hit Andy's heart. This was a terrible thing that was happening, Gram and Ellen lined up against the men. The family had always been very friendly and happy together. What was happening was nobody's fault; the women were right, and so was Gramps.

The days were slipping by and nothing was getting solved. Gram was stalling Ben Simms about buying the house, and stalling the auctioneer about the date for the sale. She and Andy didn't discuss it, but he realized that she had very little hope that Mr. Otis would be able to sell Andy's scheme to the state authorities.

Andy had asked her if she would be terribly disappointed not to move to Valley View. She had looked at him strangely, and said he obviously didn't know very much about women. How could he imagine such a thing? Yes, she liked the house in Valley View, but if she was given a real choice she would jump at the chance of staying in her own home.

The truth was, Andy and Ellen hoped the lawyer could work a miracle. Somehow, they didn't know how, they figured everything might straighten out after he went to Capitol City.

"You're just grasping at a straw," Gram warned. "Honestly, children, you're asking too much. The state won't do it."

On Wednesday the blow fell. Mr. Otis made the trip to Capitol City and the highway commissioner turned him down cold.

Andy called home soon after the lunch period, to

find out if Gram had heard anything. She sounded so queer he asked, "What's the matter, Gram? Your voice sounds funny."

"I suppose it does." She told him that the lawyer's trip had ended in failure. "Andy, I've just about come to the end of my rope," she said. "The only thing I've got to be glad about is that we never told your grandfather about that crazy scheme. It was crazy, Andy, to expect those men to go to such lengths to help us."

She didn't go on, and Andy realized she was fighting for self-control. The thought of her breaking down completely scared him as badly as he had been scared by anything during the past hard weeks. "Gram, I'm coming home," he said. "I'm not doing myself any good staying here, I'm not learning anything. I'll explain to the teacher."

"Oh, Andy, could you?" The relief in her voice made Andy realize how much she depended on him.

He asked Miss Miller to come out in the hall so he could explain. "Take the rest of the week," she suggested. "Your marks are good and you can easily make up the work. I'll tell the principal I'm excusing you because of an emergency at home."

Andy was in luck, and a ride came along soon after he started to thumb. When he walked into the yard he knew he had done the right thing. Gram had more troubles than she could manage. Mr. Grabowski's truck was backed up to the kitchen door, and he and his oldest son were waiting for Gram's orders. Gramps sat in his usual place on the overturned keg in the sunny doorway of the barn, Toby at his feet. "That

116

old fool refuses to lift a finger to help," Gram snapped.

"What's going on?" Andy asked.

Gram straightened her back and seemed to get hold of herself. "Forget what I said," she told Andy. "He may be an old fool, but he's the only husband I've got. My trouble is, I've been pushed as far as I can go. Now let's help the Grabowskis. They're going to store some of the furniture in their hay barn, until we get a place to live."

Andy and Albert Grabowski started wrestling the dining room sideboard out through the kitchen. Mr. Grabowski took one end, and the three heaved it into the back of the truck. Gramps continued to sit and watch them carrying out the chairs and tables. Finally Gram couldn't stand it any longer. "You don't deserve good neighbors!" she yelled at him. "Why should we do all the work? Come and help."

He didn't get mad. He grinned as he sauntered over. "You're going to all this trouble for nothing, Ivor," he told the farmer. "We're not leaving this house, so eventually we'll have to move all this stuff back in. If you just want to humor my wife, that's all right." He helped too, then, until the truck was full.

He and Andy hopped in back and rode to the next farm, and they all unloaded the furniture and covered it with tarpaulins. Mrs. Grabowski came out with a pitcher of lemonade, and they sat on a long bench by the kitchen door to visit.

"Listen," Gramps suddenly ordered, putting up his hand.

"I don't hear anything," Andy said.

118

"That's the point, sonny. Those confounded machines have stopped again."

They all went to find out what was going on. From a rise they could see how the machines had chewed up the landscape, leaving trees to lie where they fell, clawing through underbrush and across the open fields right to the edge of Mount Tom Road. Now the earthmovers and front-end loaders and bulldozers were lined up like yellow, prehistoric monsters on the fill that bridged the lowland. Mount Tom Brook flowed sluggishly through the giant tile. The workmen had gone away.

When the machines started moving again they would cut through the last wall. They would cross the road and attack the Wheelers' east boundary.

Andy glanced at his grandfather. Gramps' face was somber. His own farm, his fields, his outbuildings lay there, tranquil, bathed in the golden light of the afternoon. Gramps, like Andy, was thinking how for a hundred and fifty years the Wheelers had cared for the land, fed it and tilled it and loved it. Now the enemy was massed at its border.

Mr. Grabowski tried to clear his throat, as though there was a lump in it he couldn't swallow. "Mr. Wheeler, maybe you've been right all along," he said in a low voice. "Maybe my sons and I should have held out too. If we had all faced them and fought them together, we might have won."

"Father, that's ridiculous!" Albert burst out. "They're stronger than we are because they've got the law on their side."

The older men paid no attention to Albert. "It's a terrible thing, what men do to the earth," Gramps said. "It's like what war does."

"I know," his neighbor told him. "My country, Poland, has been fought over for centuries, armies coming, armies going, ravaging and destroying."

"Nowadays the young people think that progress is the only thing," Gramps said. "They think speed is so wonderful. We know differently, Ivor. This progress that people admire so much exacts an awful price."

The older men got up and walked together down the road. At the gate Mr. Grabowski shook Gramps' hand, before they parted.

"He's a nice man, isn't he?" Andy said to make conversation, as they started up the lane.

Gramps wasn't listening. "Whose car is that?" he asked, and hastened his steps.

The sheriff was standing beside the car when they reached the yard.

XII

"Why did you let him in?" Gramps yelled at Gram, who was on the back porch.

"Because in the first place you left your precious gate unlocked," she said. "Because in the second place you and I have been friends with Charlie Holmes all our lives and I see no reason to change now. Because thirdly and fourthly and fifthly I've still got all my buttons, George Wheeler. I'm not mad as a March hare, like some people I could name!"

"George, let's be friends again," the sheriff said. He made the mistake of smiling and putting out his hand as he walked toward Gramps.

Gramps stopped in his tracks, standing his ground like a balky mule, glaring.

"George, this is serious," Mr. Holmes said. "In only two days they're coming to put you out of your house, man! You've carried this thing as far as you can, so won't you drop it now? Please use some sense . . ."

"Andy, the sheriff is leaving," Gramps broke in. "Close the gate after him and put on the padlock and bring the key to me."

The sheriff and Gram looked at each other and

121

shrugged. "All right, Andy, get in and I'll give you a ride out to the road," Mr. Holmes offered.

"No, thanks, I'd rather walk," Andy told him.

Despite the rebuff the sheriff got out of the car to speak to Andy again, at the gate. "It breaks my heart to see what your grandparents are going through," he said. "You're the apple of your grandfather's eye, Andy. He worshiped your dad, and he sees your dad all over again, in you. I've got a feeling that if he'd listen to anybody in the world, it would be to you. Won't you try to persuade him to give in peaceably?"

Ellen and Andy had been trained to respect their elders, but Andy had to go against that training now. "No, I won't waste my breath," he said. "The law is wrong and Gramps is right. I'm on his side."

The sheriff sighed. "When stubbornness was handed out you Wheelers surely got your full share," he said, and drove away.

Andy had to give Ellen credit; she worked hard, right along with Gram. Andy didn't offer to help and they didn't ask him. All the family got for food was sandwiches. The women worked feverishly, tying up books, wrapping china and glass in newspapers and stuffing it in cartons, filling boxes with all the family's possessions.

Andy stood it as long as he could, feeling more and more miserable as he watched them. Then, when he saw his grandmother wrestling with a heavy box, he had to give in. He carried it to the back porch and put it with the others. "Where's this stuff going?" he asked.

"The Grabowskis and the Brookses are storing it for us. We won't need anything for a while. I've engaged rooms at the Sunset Motel. We can take our meals at the restaurant."

"Who's 'we'?"

"We is the four of us, Andy," she said. "We're split right down the middle now by a difference of opinion, but after Friday, regardless of how it turns out, we'll be together again and we'll start acting like a family."

Gramps looked amused as he watched the activity, and although he didn't help he didn't hinder. Once he said mildly, "Emily, you aren't leaving the boy and me very well fixed to keep house. You don't have to strip the place bare."

"Where we're going we won't need anything," Gram told him. "For once in my life I'll have my meals set before me, cooked and served by somebody else. They say the food's real good at that Sunset Motel."

"You sound as though I never took you to the hotel to eat," Gramps said. "You sound as though you never had a fancy honeymoon in Atlantic City. And how about that week when we went to Chicago?"

"That was a long time ago."

Gramps' blue eyes clouded. "Doesn't this house mean anything at all to you, Emily?" he pleaded.

"George, you know how it hurts me to break up my home. It's breaking my heart!" Gram wailed.

He took her in his arms, murmuring, "There, there." Anybody would think that after that one or the other would have to give in, but neither did. Gram went right on with her packing and Gramps continued to watch.

Ellen was the one who broke. They all went upstairs at ten, tired out, and Andy was in bed when his sister walked into his room without knocking. It really shook him, the fierce way she went at him. "I'd never have dreamed you could act so mean!" she accused, glaring down at him. "The day after tomorrow those machines are going to bulldoze the walls of this house right down, and you act as though it's a joke!"

"Are you nuts?" he said. "They're not going to doze the house down on Friday."

"Yes, they are. That's what the paper says."

"What paper? The newspaper didn't say anything like that."

"That legal paper did, the one Gram saved after Gramps tore the others up."

"I don't believe it," Andy said. "I know it isn't true. They'd give us plenty of time to get our stuff out, even if they were going to knock down the house, which they're not."

His voice rose. "Can't you see what'll happen, you dope? When they find out we mean business and won't give in, they'll change the highway."

Ellen was bright enough, and spotted the flaw in his argument. She lowered her voice so their grandparents wouldn't come and interrupt, but she pounced on Andy's error. "So why did you talk to Mr. Otis, and why did he go to the capital to see the commissioner?" she asked. "How about your lovely plan for the state to make us a road and move the house? You know as well as I do that the bulldozers mean business, and they'll knock this house down so not one stone will stand on another."

Her face was working and she let out a bellow of grief. "Oh, you're the fool, Andy Wheeler, you're the fool!" she wailed, and ran out.

He finally drifted off to sleep after the clock had struck twelve. He awoke at daylight, thinking, Boy, this family is in a big, fat mess. He wondered, while he was pulling on dungarees and a flannel shirt, Is this the last day we'll ever spend here?

Early as it was, the old people were in the kitchen. Gram was frying eggs and bacon for her husband, because no matter how mad she was at him she couldn't let him go hungry.

Gramps gallantly got up to pour her coffee, after she had set his food before him. Then he started a fresh argument. "Have you given any thought to Toby?" he asked. "Do you reckon that fancy motel where you plan to live will take a broken-down farm dog?"

"Of course they will."

"Have you asked them?"

"No, but I know they will."

Andy hated to hear them fighting over the dog, because they both adored Toby equally. He interrupted, "Gramps, are you going to help me clean out the hen house this morning?"

Gramps was startled, for this was Andy's chore, not

his, but he agreed. Then he added, "I'll help you wash the hens, too. Each and every one of 'em is going to have a bath. Of course they may get pneumonia out of it but we can't let your grandma and Ellen take a bunch of dirty hens with them to their Sunset Motel."

Ellen had come down, and she heard. "You think you're funny, don't you?" she demanded fiercely. "You know the Grabowskis are buying the hens. You think this whole thing is just a joke!"

The telephone kept ringing all morning. Several people just wanted to talk; their curiosity about what was going on at the Wheeler place got the better of them. Gramps' friend Harned Brooks called to remind Gramps that he was keeping an eagle eye on the road. He would give the warning when any hostile enemy passed his place, the enemy being the sheriff and the police.

Gramps hovered near the telephone, and once when it rang he summoned Gram, "It's your boyfriend."

Whenever the two engaged in a battle of wits Gram always gave back as good as she received. "Which boyfriend?" she asked. "I've got so many you'll have to identify him better than that."

"It's your auctioneer friend," Gramps told her.

Evidently Mr. Metcalf begged her to set a date for the sale. She listened for a minute and then her voice rose. "I know we're going to be put out on the road, Ham. That's no news to me. Very well, we'll hold the auction in the middle of the road but I still can't tell you when!" She hung up.

126

Gramps finally admitted to Andy why he was sticking so close to the phone. "I put in a call to that Associated Press feller," he said. "I want to make sure he'll be here tomorrow. We mustn't let your grandmother answer. She'd tell him to stay away and mind his own business, and we want him."

Luckily Mr. Singer returned Gramps' call while Gram was upstairs. Andy gathered that the reporter agreed to come the next day. "Are you bringing a camera to take a motion picture?" Gramps asked, and grinned broadly, for evidently Mr. Singer said he planned to.

Gramps' attitude really troubled Andy. Wasn't he acting like what Gram had called him once, "a senile old man"? He accused his grandfather of that. "Honestly, anybody would think you were a real publicity hound, Gramps," he said. "Anybody would think you liked this business, your name in the paper and all that. Why do you want a movie camera here?"

His grandfather didn't get angry, as he had every right to do. He took Andy by the arm and led him out of the house. "Son, I'm not seeking publicity for myself," he said. "You and I agreed, when this thing started, that a man has to fight for what he believes in. In this case it's a man's right to defend his own home, remember?

"Sometimes a trouble builds and builds and gets bigger and bigger, and that's the case here. It would be mighty easy to turn tail and run, give in and move off our land and leave it to the despoilers. But you and I aren't doing that. We're sticking until the last gun is fired, right? And we want the camera here, we need it, so the whole world will see that some folks are still ready and willing and able to fight for their rights."

He was anxiously watching Andy's face. Andy couldn't think what to say. He was suddenly flooded with love and pride in this cantankerous, stubborn old man. "Isn't that the case, Andy?" Gramps seemed to be begging for reassurance.

"Yes, that's the case, Gramps," Andy said. "We'll stick, like you say, and it's all right about Mr. Singer and the camera and all."

"But our womenfolks have to be gone," Gramps said. "Bright and early tomorrow morning Harned Brooks is coming to take them to his place. Oh, nothing very terrible is going to happen. I don't mean they'd be in any danger. Just the same, we want them off the place."

"Okay."

"This isn't a proper kind of a fight for women."

It crossed Andy's mind that maybe it wasn't a proper kind of a fight for an eleven-year-old kid and a seventy-three-year-old man, either. They seemed rather an inadequate force to hold off a bunch of policemen and a lot of state officials. He didn't mention this, though, he just said, "Right-o."

They proceeded to do what they had to do, through the long hours of Thursday. The women went on with their packing. The four were oddly tender and thoughtful of one another, but there was very little talking.

128

Andy stuck close to Gramps. There had been times during the past months when he had felt as though he was the stronger of the two, but that feeling was gone today. His fragile, white-haired grandfather looked to him like a tower of strength.

The gate was locked. The rifle hung where it always had, on the pegs over the coatrack in the back entry. It was cleaned and loaded. Every time he glanced at it Andy felt nervous flutters in his stomach.

He didn't have to ask, he knew his grandfather was the one who would handle the gun. He did ask, though, "Gramps, isn't there any sort of an old gun I could have, even if it wasn't loaded, or wouldn't fire if it was?"

"I never had a revolver," Gramps said, "and we never got you the BB gun you thought you wanted, a year or so ago. Your Gram is so dead set against the killing of birds and squirrels, or even varmints like woodchucks, she wouldn't let me put a gun in your hands."

He was thoughtful, gazing across the fields at the far hills. Then he said quietly, "It isn't going to come to that, Andy. You won't need a gun, tomorrow or any other day."

Andy thought to himself, I wish I was sure of that too, but he made no answer. He couldn't argue with this calm, purposeful man.

The telephone kept on ringing, and finally toward night it got to be such a nuisance Gram took it off the hook. They had finished supper, and Andy had gone outside to make sure Toby had fresh water and food and was bedded down in the barn, when he heard a car horn honking. In the half-light he saw Bill Otis running toward the house.

"It's my Dad back there, making all the racket," he said, when Andy met him in the lane. "We couldn't get you on the phone. Dad wanted to tell your grandmother he's driving to Capitol City again, tomorrow morning. He made another date with the highway commissioner. If he doesn't get satisfaction from the commissioner he's going to try to see the governor. Tell your grandmother that, will you?"

"All right."

"Oh, golly," Bill groaned.

"Golly what?"

"I wish I didn't have to go to school tomorrow. I tried to argue my folks into letting me stay home. I want to be here."

"It isn't going to be any picnic," Andy said.

"Who says it's going to be a picnic? I just want to be here."

"I sure wish you could," Andy told him. "So long."

XIII

NOBODY SLEPT MUCH that night. Andy lay awake listening to his grandparents' voices, down the hall. Tired as they were, they argued for hours. Once Ellen cried out, and Gram went to comfort her.

Andy was surprised to open his eyes and find broad daylight, so he knew he had slept a little. He didn't hear anyone moving when he dressed and tiptoed downstairs.

Gram sat at the kitchen table, stirring her coffee, staring out of the window. There were black circles under her eyes. "You don't look as though you'd slept at all," Andy said.

"Maybe I catnapped some."

"I heard you talking."

"I've agreed to leave," Gram said. "I'm taking Ellen, and we'll be at Ruth Brooks' house. I want you to go with us, but I'm not going to insist."

"Gram, you're not scared of what will happen today, are you?"

"Scared of your getting hurt physically?" Gram asked. "No, Andy, I'm not. But I wish I knew what that terrible old man plans to do."

Neither was aware that Gramps was listening outside the screen door. "That terrible old man plans to eat his breakfast, that's what," Gramps said. "Woman, get busy and cook it. I called Harned and asked him to fetch you early."

"That suits me fine!" Gram snapped, her face reddening. "I'm glad to leave. I never want to set foot in this house again."

"And that suits me fine!" Gramps fired back at her. "The last thing Andy and I need around here is a bunch of disloyal females."

He seemed to be in high spirits while they ate the meal that Gram grimly set before them. They were just finishing when Mr. Brooks arrived. Gramps rushed Ellen and Gram out to the car.

"Leave those dishes," he ordered, coming back in and finding Andy at the sink. "That's women's work. We've got more important things on our minds."

Andy paid no attention but went ahead. Gram had always taken great pride in her home, and he couldn't bear to let strangers walk in and find dirty dishes in the sink. Afterward he wandered through the house. His footsteps echoed, for the rooms were bare.

One minute his heart was in his shoes and he felt so depressed he only wanted to shut himself up alone somewhere and cry. The next he felt exhilarated and excited, really high.

A clatter out on the main road caught his attention; a big machine was moving. Andy raced outdoors and down the lane.

The rest of the road equipment stood where the men had left it, lined up along the last cut across the Grabowski land. One bulldozer was approaching, so big it looked about twenty feet high. Andy watched it advance through the wall that edged the road, pushing the boulders aside as though they were chunks of foam. It clanked across Mount Tom Road and nosed into the turf, its huge blade only three feet from the corner of the Wheelers' boundary.

Andy jumped in front of it, waving his arms. "Stop, stop!"

The operator cut the switch and leaned back in his seat. "The boss told me I'd meet opposition, but I expected more than one skinny kid," he said. "Are you the Wheeler boy?"

"Yes, and you keep that machine off our land!"

"I aim to," the man said mildly. "My boss and I came out last night, and he showed me where I was to park this 'dozer. You've got no complaints. I stopped before I touched your land."

"Now what are you going to do?" Andy demanded.

"I'm going to sit here, nice and easy, until my boss tells me to proceed."

He was a big man with a friendly face, and Andy had a feeling he would like him very much, if circumstances were different. Andy couldn't give in though and be friendly, not today. He scowled and said, "You be mighty careful you don't move that thing one foot farther," and stalked away.

He shook the gate and examined the padlock, to make sure everything was all right. He found the chair

133

which his grandfather had hidden in the tall weeds, and set it up in the middle of the lane. This was where Gramps planned to do battle. Then he went back to the house.

The kitchen clock struck ten. Gramps greeted him from the porch, "My lookout, Harned Brooks, just called to tell us the reporter feller is on his way. Suppose we go to meet him."

Toby joined them, tail wagging, but the last thing they needed with them that day was a lame, old dog that liked to growl at strangers. Andy hustled him back to the barn and snapped his chain.

Gramps had slicked down his hair and buttoned the collar of his shirt. He looked strong and purposeful as he marched along, the rifle laid across his arm. Andy thought, He walks like the general of an army. Then he thought, Some army, just me!

A light panel truck drew up. Gramps wouldn't open the gate, so Mr. Singer climbed over it. "What are our plans, Mr. Wheeler?" he asked. "Do we just wait all day?"

"I guess so," Gramps said. He was glaring in the direction of the bulldozer, and Andy explained that the operator was there on orders from his boss, and didn't intend to start any trouble. The man waved, but Gramps only glowered back.

"Where's your camera?" he asked Mr. Singer. "Don't tell me you didn't bring it."

"The cameraman and the sound man are waiting in the truck," Mr. Singer explained. "They figure they might as well catch up on their sleep, and I think I'll join them and do the same." He climbed back over the gate.

It was a real weird situation. Andy sat on the ground near Gramps, who perched bolt upright on his chair, cradling the rifle. The bulldozer driver put his head down on his arms and seemed to be asleep, and so, apparently, were the men in the panel truck. We could wait all day and nothing could happen, Andy realized.

An hour passed. Gramps too was nodding when Andy put a hand on his arm. "They're coming," he whispered. He had heard the rumble of cars climbing Dog Leg Hill.

The first was a pickup truck, careening wildly along the country road. It braked to a stop with a squeal of tires and Mr. Brooks tumbled out. "They're coming, they're coming!" he shouted.

Andy and Gramps advanced to the gate to meet him. "Calm down, Harned," Gramps advised. "You're not Paul Revere!"

A second car followed. The boss of the road gang jumped out and joined the 'dozer driver.

Mr. Singer and his companions took up positions across the road, where the camera had a clear view. The sheriff's car drew up. The next two were full of state police. The men assembled and approached the gate, and to Andy it looked like a full company of troops.

The sheriff leaned his arm on the gate and hopefully grinned across it. "Take yourself off my property," Gramps ordered, brandishing the gun.

"Now, now, George," Mr. Holmes said soothingly, as though he was addressing a child, "you've had your fun, so let's stop playing games, shall we?"

"Are you fellers taking pictures of this?" Gramps called. Mr. Singer nodded.

"All right, now," Gramps said briskly. "You're the one who's had his fun, Sheriff Holmes. "You've made your show, you've brought the minions of the

law to threaten me and my grandson with bodily
harm."

A state policeman came forward, and Andy saw the
bars on his shoulder and the word "Captain" on his
badge. He too was smiling, to let the Wheelers know
he wasn't taking the situation too seriously. "Mr.
Wheeler, don't you think this affair has gone far
enough?" he asked.

"Not as far as it'll go if you or one of your fancy cops pushes on my gate, or that bulldozer man sets his blade on my soil."

Sheriff Holmes appealed to Andy, "Haven't you and your grandma had any luck at all, winning him around to facing the facts?"

Gramps didn't try to put words in Andy's mouth, he let him speak for himself. Andy hesitated, afraid his voice would break and show how scared he was of the group of men who faced him. "I haven't tried," he said. "My grandfather knows what he's doing, and I agree with him a hundred percent."

The sheriff sighed. "All right, men, do what you came to do," he ordered.

The police came forward. Three of them steadied the gate while another struck the padlock with a hammer, trying to break it loose from the chain that circled the post.

Andy was standing directly behind his grandfather. "Don't, don't," he whispered.

Gramps was sighting along the barrel of the rifle. All could hear the metallic click as he shot the bolt, bringing the bullet into firing position. His long, index finger closed around the trigger. "Step back from the gate." His voice was deadly calm.

The rifle poised in midair, the hammer at the ready. The police didn't move, they didn't take their hands off the top bar of the gate. Andy, behind Gramps, sighted along the barrel of the gun. It was aimed at the captain's chest.

Neither of the Wheelers moved, or even glanced

away, although they heard the rumble of a car. It stopped at the gate, and Gram got out, followed by Ellen. Their faces were stiff and expressionless. The men parted to let them through. "George, open the gate for us," Gram commanded.

Her voice was a voice of authority, and when she gave an order in a certain steady tone, her family obeyed. Now the gun wavered. Andy reached around his grandfather and took it.

Gramps put the key in the lock, muttering because the padlock was bent. It finally worked, and Gramps took down the chain and the women slipped through. "Now, George, put the chain back," Gram ordered.

A marvelous feeling of happiness surged through Andy. The family was together again. As for Gramps, his face glowed. "You had to come back, Emily," he said. "You couldn't stay away."

Gram took her place beside her husband, facing the crowd. "All right, George, you're the boss," she said.

Ellen's hand slipped into Andy's, and he gave it a quick squeeze. "I'm glad you're here to help us hold the fort," he whispered.

Gramps was in command, and what was he going to do? Andy still held the rifle. He hoped and prayed Gramps wouldn't ask for it back, but like the women he waited for Gramps to make his move.

The scene was absolutely still. Nobody spoke. An oriole sang in the maple tree over their heads, and when it stopped they could hear the whirr of the motion picture camera. All were waiting.

Gramps' back was ramrod stiff, and his face was pale but proud. He took his wife's arm and swung around, and never looked back as he marched up the lane to the house. The children followed.

Nobody turned to see what happened, but they heard. The hammer struck the padlock, the chain rattled, the gate squeaked as it swung open. The sheriff spoke a command and the bulldozer roared. Andy didn't have to see; he knew that the machine advanced and took its first bite into his grandparents' land.

There was nothing to say, for they had lost. It was noon, and from force of habit Gram proceeded to fix a meal. She and the children anxiously watched Gramps.

He sat at the table, thoughtfully staring out of the window. He didn't look hurt, or feeble, or defeated. They picked up spoons and began to eat their soup.

Suddenly, tongues were loosened. "We put up a pretty fair fight," Andy mentioned.

Gramps growled in his throat. "It was these interfering females who wrecked everything. If they hadn't showed up I'd have shot the lot of those police!"

"Gramps, you wouldn't have done any such thing," Ellen protested, shocked.

"Do you want to bet?" Andy asked.

Gram laughed. "Your grandfather was licked before he started," she said. "He couldn't use that gun against anything, a man or any living thing. Children, don't you remember the day he decided to shoot the swallows in the barn, because they were messing up the farm gear with their droppings? He went out there and he snorted and he swore but he couldn't pull the trigger. Those swallows are still out there messing up the place."

There was a light tap at the screen door. "I just came to say good-bye," Mr. Singer called.

Gramps went to speak to him. "I'm sorry you didn't get your story," he said. "The way it turned out, you came all the way up here for nothing. My womenfolks spoiled everything. I'd hoped to provide your camera feller with pictures of state policemen lying all over the place in pools of blood."

"That's all right, Mr. Wheeler," the reporter said. "We got our story. Good-bye."

The telephone was ringing, and Andy was nearest. "I'll get my grandfather," he said, recognizing the sheriff's voice.

Sheriff Holmes protested nervously, "No, no, Andy, you can give him the message. Just tell him the state's allowing him an extra month to remove from the premises. And Andy, tell him I hope there aren't any real hard feelings between him and me."

Andy relayed the message to Gram, for his grandfather had walked outside. "I should have thanked him, but I didn't," Andy said. "Giving us an extra month isn't doing us much of a favor. I mean, it's going to be a real rough month for all of us. It would have been easier if they'd just put us off the place, so the whole thing was over."

"I know, I know," Gram said. "Now go after your grandfather, son. I don't want him to be alone."

XIV

Gʀᴀᴍᴘꜱ ᴄᴀᴍᴇ ʙᴀᴄᴋ meekly enough when Andy went after him. The fight seemed to be completely gone out of him. He listened and nodded and said nothing when Ellen tried to wheedle him, putting her arms around him and telling him how he was going to love the house in Valley View. He picked at his food at suppertime, and soon afterward went up to his room.

He still had a dazed look in his eyes when he came down the next morning. He drank his coffee and again left his food untouched. Soon he got up and pulled on a sweater and went outdoors. Gram didn't have to suggest it; Andy waited until Gramps had a head start, and then followed.

He crossed the north lots, watching Gramps climbing Mount Tom. He passed a new mound of earth and judged it must have been a giant woodchuck who had dug such a big hole.

His mind registered the fact that he must remember to bring a shovel and fill it in, the next time he went that way. Then he remembered that it didn't matter if the woodchucks took over the place. After the state put through the road, his grandparents would sell what was left of the land.

The land would never be the same, now that the herd was gone. Andy's alert eyes noted cedar seedlings springing up from the turf. Mr. Grabowski pastured his stock in these fenced fields all summer, and the cows kept the grass down but wouldn't touch the small cedars. Soon they would shoot up to real trees. They and the woodchucks together would take over the land.

Everything changed, Andy knew. People grew older and life was different. This was one change that hurt him deeply and personally. Six generations of Wheelers had tended and loved these acres, and soon they would go back to the wild.

He reached the brook and crossed by the stepping stones. Gramps saw him and waved, and stopped to wait. Andy joined him on their favorite lookout boulder. Neither spoke, for there was nothing they could say that wouldn't hurt.

The old folks' hearts, and Ellen's too, were just as lacerated and sore as his, Andy knew. The same sadness gripped them all.

Maybe he was the luckiest, Andy realized. He had a good future ahead of him. If he worked hard enough and got a few breaks, he might have a career in baseball. That was all in the years ahead, though. It didn't help much now.

He watched a car turn in at the open gate and stop behind the house. "I won't go down," Gramps said. "There's not a soul in the world I want to talk to."

The triangle sounded loud and clear; somebody was vigorously whacking it with the iron rod. "Gram wouldn't tell Ellen to bang on that thing if it wasn't important," Andy said.

"I suppose," Gramps agreed reluctantly, and slid off the rock.

Andy let down the last set of bars for his grandfather, and straightened up to see better. "It's Mr. Otis' car," he said.

"I don't mean any disrespect to him because he's a nice chap, but what could he have to say that we want to hear?" Gramps asked. "It's too late, it's all over. We'll auction off our belongings and move into that blasted development. But regardless of what the minister says, I'll never forgive my enemies . . ."

"Gramps, we could build ourselves a house," Andy interrupted, to stop the tirade.

"Where?"

"Up on the hill. We don't have to sell the upper land."

"How would we get up there? Fly?"

"We could borrow money from the bank if we had to, and put in a road," Andy patiently pointed out.

"We'd be snowbound all winter."

"No, we wouldn't. We'd buy a plow attachment for the tractor and I'd plow us out."

"Who wants a new house, the kind they build nowadays?" Gramps demanded.

"They build good houses nowadays."

"No they don't, what they build is ramshackle, jerry-built, put together with tacks and spit! You

144

think that's what we want, a shack set in the middle of a hill with no shade? Where we'd have to watch those danged cars and trucks going past at sixty miles an hour?"

"Come on, Gramps, stir your stumps," Andy ordered. "We can't just stand here all day. We could build a good house and you know it, and we'd set it in a clump of trees for shade."

Gramps lifted his face and wailed, "I don't want a new house, I want my own home!"

Andy put his arms around him, as he would have around a child. "I know, I know, Gramps. Now let's talk to Mr. Otis. We have to be polite to him because he's really tried to help us."

Andy couldn't believe what he saw in his grandmother's face, when he opened the door. It glowed with pure joy, as though a lamp had gone on behind it. Mr. Otis was smiling and Ellen looked as though she was ready to burst. "What's happened?" Andy stammered.

"Mr. Wheeler," the lawyer began.

"Mr. Otis, let me tell," Gram begged. "George, what would you say if you knew we were going to stay in our own house? If our house was set so it faced what you've always declared is the finest view in the whole United States?"

"What do you mean?" Gramps demanded.

"That's what's going to happen!"

Andy's voice shook. "Are you trying to tell us they've changed their minds and they're going to move the house?"

"Yes, and the nasty old state is paying for the whole thing!" Ellen shouted.

"Now you can explain, please," Gram told Mr. Otis.

"That's the situation, Mr. Wheeler," the lawyer began. "The state has made you a counter offer. They'll give you half the cash sum set at the condemnation hearing, for the portion of your land they need for the highway. They'll pay the total cost of digging out a new road a quarter mile long. Your wife thinks that would reach the lower slope of Andy's mountain."

Andy's ears pricked up. Why had the lawyer called it that? In his secret thoughts Andy had sometimes thought of it that way, but he had never said the words aloud.

"The state will put the house on rollers and transport it and place it wherever you want it placed." Mr. Otis went on.

"We don't even have to get out," Ellen added. "We can live right in our own home while it's being moved."

The lawyer stood up. "I'll go along and leave you to talk it over."

Gram hugged him and thanked him. They all tagged after him out to his car. He looked very contented, when he leaned back in the seat. "This has been a good day's work," he said.

"It was all your work," Andy pointed out.

"No, young man, you Wheelers did it."

"We didn't have anything to do with those men at

Capitol City changing their minds," Andy said, confused.

"You people made them change their minds." All the Wheelers looked puzzled. "They saw the broadcast on television last night," the lawyer explained.

"What broadcast?" Andy asked.

It was Mr. Otis's turn to look surprised. "Are you telling me you missed it?" he asked. "I took it for granted you had seen it. You were all on the six o'clock news, Andy, you and your grandfather holding off the police, and then giving in when Ellen and your grandmother came. The reporter, Mr. Singer, told how all you wanted was to stay in your home, how you wished it could be moved up on Andy's mountain."

"Why do you call it that?" Gram asked.

"It's what Mr. Singer called it. Anyway, the whole thing was quite moving. As a matter of fact, my wife cried."

"We never thought to turn on the TV," Gram explained. "We were all so tired, it never occurred to us."

"Probably about a million people in this state saw it," Mr. Otis said. "The governor was one of them. Apparently his home was besieged by angry telephone calls. He's up for reelection next fall, and he realized that this is a human interest story that could be used against him — the hard-hearted state putting people out on the road and destroying their beautiful, old home.

"The governor called the highway commissioner,

147

and the commissioner contacted me about eleven o'clock last night, asking me to be at his office early this morning. I didn't want to raise any false hopes, so I didn't get in touch with you. The commissioner will have papers drawn up, outlining their offer. So that's the whole story."

Mr. Otis turned his car, and was about to drive down the lane when he stopped and backed up. "The commissioner did ask one thing of you," he said. "Last night's publicity has hurt the governor's administration, so he'd like a little good publicity to get back the popularity he's lost. He asks that you let the news people come for another interview, and more pictures, after the house is moved and you're living up on the hill. All right?"

"All right, fine!" they shouted in chorus. He was laughing as he drove off.

The Wheelers swung around. Nobody asked where the four were going. They crossed the north meadows and the brook, Andy helping his grandfather, who still seemed bewildered and disbelieving. It wasn't until they reached the level spot, below the boulder, that they found their tongues. "Are we going to change the name of the mountain?" Ellen asked.

"No, of course not. Don't be a dope," Andy said. "It's always been Mount Tom, and it always will be Mount Tom. This is the spot where we ought to put the house."

Below lay the farm, and the raw wound in the earth that would heal after the highway was finished. Beyond, the hills lay fold on blue fold to the horizon.

148

The sun, swinging across the sky, would wash their house in sunlight, and the graceful birches and the tall oak would give it shade.

"Who says this is the spot?" Ellen demanded.

"Andy says," Gram announced. "The whole solution was his idea. Right, Ellen?"

"Okay," Ellen agreed.

"Right, George?"

"Right!" Gramps shouted. He gave Andy such a whack on the back Andy almost fell flat on his face. "This boy is pure Wheeler. Who but a Wheeler would think of a smart deal like this?"

"Yeah!" Andy yelled. His heart suddenly swelled

like a balloon and there was no room inside him for anything but happiness. "There's nobody as smart as us Wheelers. We're like the turtles that go around with their houses on their backs, we pick up our house and carry it up the mountain!"

They laughed and laughed, and Gramps seized Gram and swung her around and danced with her on the mossy hill. "Stop this, you old fool," Gram said finally, gasping for breath.

Andy had the last word. He said as they started down the slope, "Gramps, we lost the battle but we won the war."

They turned those words into a tune, and sang them all the way down the mountain.

100193